A TLA Spirit of Texas Reading List Selection
A VOYA Top Shelf Selection
A Dorothy Canfield Fisher Master List Selection
A Kansas NEA Reading Circle Master List Selection

An Amazon Best Book of the Year
A VOYA Perfect Ten

★ "Artfully told." —*School Library Journal*, starred review
★ "A novel that sings from the heart." —*VOYA*, starred review

THE
LOST BOY'S
GIFT

KIMBERLY WILLIS HOLT

with illustrations by **Jonathan Bean**

Christy Ottaviano Books
Henry Holt and Company
New York

Henry Holt and Company, *Publishers since 1866*
Henry Holt® is a registered trademark of Macmillan Publishing Group, LLC
175 Fifth Avenue, New York, New York 10010 • mackids.com

Library of Congress Cataloging-in-Publication Data
Names: Holt, Kimberly Willis, author. | Bean, Jonathan, 1979– illustrator.
Title: The Lost Boy's gift / Kimberly Willis Holt ; with illustrations by Jonathan Bean.
Description: First edition. | New York : Henry Holt and Company, 2019. | "Christy Ottaviano
Books." | Summary: When his parents separate, Daniel very unhappily moves to a cottage on
While-a-Way Lane, but neighbor Tilda Butter helps him discover he has a special gift like hers.
Identifiers: LCCN 2018039237 | ISBN 9781627793261 (hardcover)
Subjects: | CYAC: Moving, Household—Fiction. | Neighborhoods—Fiction. | Human-Animal
communication—Fiction. | Schools—Fiction. | Theater—Fiction. | Family problems—Fiction.
Classification: LCC PZ7.H74023 Los 2019 | DDC [Fic]—dc23
LC record available at https://lccn.loc.gov/2018039237

Our books may be purchased in bulk for promotional, educational, or business use.
Please contact your local bookseller or the Macmillan Corporate and Premium Sales Department
at (800) 221-7945 ext. 5442 or by email at MacmillanSpecialMarkets@macmillan.com.

First edition, 2019 / Designed by Patrick Collins
Printed in the United States of America by LSC Communications, Harrisonburg, Virginia

1 3 5 7 9 10 8 6 4 2

for Christy Ottaviano

1. Green Things
2. Etc. Etc.
3. Tooth Fairy Dentistry
4. Pie World
5. This 'n' That Street
6. Pancake Palace
7. Fly Me to the Moon
   Kite Shop
8. Fine Feathered Friends
9. Penny's Pogo Stick Store
10. Library
11. Falling Star Valley School
12. Falling Star Valley
    University
13. Wit's End Street
14. Think Tank
15. Annie's cottage
16. Agatha Brown's cottage
17. Dewey Wonder's
    childhood home
18. While-a-Way Lane
19. Annie's lemonade stand
20. Dewey Wonder's
    cottage
21. The pond
22. Tilda Butter's cottage
23. Daniel's cottage

THE
LOST BOY'S
GIFT

CHAPTER ONE

A WORLD AWAY

THERE ARE PLACES where you want to go and places where you want to leave. There are also places where you want to stay. Sometimes you have no choice in the matter. This was the case for a boy named Daniel, who was moving to a street called While-a-Way Lane.

Daniel was trying to pack, but how do you pack when you don't want to leave?

Only some of his stuff was going to their new house because his mother said it was a lot smaller. A cottage, she called it. All week, Daniel tried to pick his favorite things. He started with his rock collection, dumping it into a box. Then he tossed in his slingshot and his skateboard. He packed the only book worth reading, *Peter Pan*.

The stuffed animals lay crammed in the back of the closet. He'd grown too old for them. One at a time, he threw them across the room, aiming for the donation box. Maybe this wouldn't be hard after all. Then he came to Snappy, his stuffed snail. His parents had thought it was funny how he named a snail "Snappy," since snails aren't known to move at a quick pace. But he had been a little kid. How was he supposed to know?

He'd received Snappy on his fourth birthday, the same day his parents moved him to the big bedroom with the four-poster bed down the hall.

Five years ago the room had seemed so far away from his old room, and the bed had seemed huge. He'd wondered if a dragon could be hiding underneath it.

Snappy made him feel safer. Daniel liked rubbing his cheek against the soft shell. It felt like velvet. The first night he'd whispered into Snappy's antennas, "I'm scared." Snappy had seemed to understand, letting Daniel hold him tight against his chest.

He stroked the now-faded shell and took a big sniff of the familiar mustiness. Maybe he could use Snappy for a pillow. No, he wasn't a little kid anymore. He threw Snappy across the room and watched him disappear into the donation box.

Daniel took time wrapping his sailboat with Bubble Wrap. His dad had purchased the boat on a business trip in Paris, where he said people sailed those remote-controlled toys in the park ponds. He'd promised Daniel one day they would find a nearby pond and try it out.

Now everything had changed.

His dad wasn't going with them to While-a-Way Lane. Last week he moved into a condo downtown. Before his dad walked through their front door for the last time, Daniel asked if they'd still sail the boat together. His dad told him they would, that living apart wouldn't be much different. But each day that passed felt stranger.

If his mother weren't making him move to While-a-Way Lane, he wouldn't have to decide what to take and leave behind. He could stay in his home. He wouldn't have to leave behind their staircase with the handrail he slid down every morning for breakfast, and the tall tree he could climb to the very top, where he yelled, "I'm the Champ!"

Why did *she* have to change it all?

He wouldn't have to say goodbye to his friends.

Or his dad.

His mother said While-a-Way Lane was a peaceful street where you could hear the birds chirp. That sounded boring. Daniel loved the noises outside his window—the whining sirens of the fire engines and police cars, the garbage truck's loud moan, the passenger train's whistle. Those sounds made him think adventures were happening all around him. He didn't care about birds chirping. Maybe he didn't even like birds.

While-a-Way Lane may have only been across the county, but to Daniel it was a world away.

CHAPTER TWO

WHILE-A-WAY LANE

SOME OF THE THINGS that Tilda Butter loved about living on While-a-Way Lane were the sounds—the birds chirping from oak trees, the leaves rustling on windy days, even the *ping-pang*ing of Agatha Brown's piano students across the street. The sounds reminded her that While-a-Way Lane was the very best place to live.

Tilda didn't always feel that way about While-a-Way Lane. She remembered the day years ago when she was seven years old and her parents dropped her off at this very house to stay with Aunt Sippy. She watched them walk away toward the train station at the edge of town, her father in his black cape, her mother in her fur wrap. It wasn't even cold outside that day.

They were only supposed to be gone for the summer while they toured the country in their opera starring roles. But the show had been a great success and the limited run had turned into a year. Then a decade. Then another, and a few more. For all Tilda knew, her parents could still be taking curtain calls. She hadn't seen or heard from them in so long, not even on her birthdays. And there had been many, so many that she didn't bother to put candles on the cake anymore for fear that it might catch fire.

Aunt Sippy loved Tilda, though, and when she died, she left Tilda her home. This yellow cottage on While-a-Way Lane was the only home Tilda cared to remember.

The morning her new neighbors were heading to While-a-Way Lane, Tilda had bundles of things to do.

She needed to tidy the garden, wash the dishes (there were always dishes in the sink), and do the laundry (piles were always waiting). She hated housework and had no problem avoiding it. She considered it one of the best privileges of being a grown-up and living alone.

Tilda decided to have a sit in her favorite chair for a few minutes. She should have known better because whenever Tilda settled in her favorite chair, her dog, Fred, took advantage of an irresistible opportunity. A lap.

Fred loved Tilda's lap. It was soft and cushy. And her belly had a little roll around the middle that formed a pillow perfect for resting against.

There was only one problem.

Fred was not a lapdog. He was a big dog. Or to put it more exactly, he was a big dog who thought he was a lapdog.

"Oh, Freddie boy, not today."

Fred wiggled and circled atop Tilda's lap, searching for just the right direction to face.

Tilda put up with all the paw poking and tail smacking because she loved Fred.

Finally Fred curled up into a tight brown ball (as much as a very large dog is able to do), but his body still spilled over Tilda's lap with his tail brushing the floor. Now settled, he rested his chin on her head.

Whenever Fred did that, Tilda's heart melted into a puddle of cream and she said, "Only for a while, dear boy."

She stretched her arm high and scratched the spot between his ears while she craned her head around Fred, watching the comings and goings of While-a-Way Lane outside her window.

Usually at this hour there would be a child walking slowly, very slowly, to a piano lesson at Agatha Brown's home across the street, but it was spring break, and most of While-a-Way Lane was off on vacation. The newspaper deliveryman drove by Tilda's cottage and pitched the paper. It hit her front door and landed with a thump on the mat.

Fred sighed. Nothing could stir him from this bliss. But a moment later, when Dewey Wonder, the mailman, stopped and the mailbox creaked open, Fred growled and barked until he heard Dewey's jeep putter away.

You might think this all seems very ordinary, or maybe even, like Daniel, you might think While-a-Way Lane is a boring place. But you didn't look close enough.

Tilda knew how to look closely. Just as she was wondering who might be her new neighbors, a moving truck backed into the driveway next door. Three men carried item after item into the house. There were the usual sorts of things one would see when someone moves in—bed frames, mattresses, sofa, and chairs.

"This doesn't tell me anything about our new neighbors," Tilda said to Fred.

But of course, Fred didn't understand what she was saying. He just understood that Tilda had stopped scratching. He gave out a little whimper.

Tilda ignored him because she noticed one of the

men carrying a blue bicycle. The kind of bicycle a child might ride. "How nice! We will have a young family living next door!"

Fred gave Tilda a big lick on the cheek because he was now happy. Tilda was scratching him again.

CHAPTER THREE

FIRST APPEARANCE

DANIEL AND HIS MOTHER had reached Falling Star Valley, a place he'd never been. On clear days he'd caught a glimpse of the top of Pointy Mountain from his school-yard, but now here it stood, stretched out before them, guarding the valley, like a skyscraper set in the middle of the city. His mother turned on Wit's End and drove past his new school. It was just around the corner from their new house.

"Scitter bum!" Daniel mumbled. Walking distance. He enjoyed riding the city bus to his old school. Bus

333 passed a million interesting things along the way. Businesspeople rushing to work, the loud swishing of the street sweeper, the bakery window filled with stacked cakes. He could probably be at this school in five minutes. The public library was across the street from the school, and to the side of it was a Ferris wheel. It wasn't moving, though.

"That's dumb," Daniel said. "What good is a Ferris wheel if it doesn't work?" Then he saw the sign. CLOSED FOR SPRING BREAK.

When they reached While-a-Way Lane, Daniel decided there was nothing he liked about the street. It didn't matter that the neighborhood had a clear view of Pointy Mountain. The small cottages resembled dollhouses—purple, blue, yellow, and pink. Nothing like the three-story townhouse he'd lived in all his life.

Then he noticed a lemonade stand with multicolored flags strung above it. Each flag included a drawing of an animal or an insect. Daniel's mouth suddenly felt dry. There was another sign: CLOSED FOR SPRING BREAK.

"The whole town is shut down," he muttered.

They hadn't passed one kid. He rolled down the window to listen for young voices. Not a peep, but there was a whiff of cotton candy in the air. He guessed that would be okay, if he were the sort of person who liked cotton candy. Well, he liked it a little, but only when he went to a circus or a fair. He didn't want to live on a street that smelled like sticky sweet stuff.

His mother drove up to their new home. She'd forgotten to mention it was pink. At the yellow cottage next door, a lady wearing a wide straw hat was kneeling at her flower bed near the edge of the yard. A big shaggy dog lay beside her. When Daniel and his mom got out of the car, he could hear the lady talking to someone.

The dog?

No, he didn't think so. She wasn't looking at him. It seemed to Daniel she was talking to no one.

LOOK CLOSER

DANIEL WAS NOT LOOKING close enough. Tilda Butter *was* talking to someone.

A snake.

And if Daniel had looked even closer, he would have noticed the snake was talking back.

TEA WITH A SPIDER

TILDA BUTTER SMILED and waved at the new neighbors. The woman raised her hand, but she didn't smile back. The boy looked the other way. They walked slowly to their new home as if they wanted to be somewhere else, as if they were dreading opening the door.

"What do you sssupposse that'sss all about?" Isadora asked. Even from the ground, a snake notices what is going on above.

"Not quite sure," Tilda said. She decided it was best to wait for introductions.

RAIN PATTERED ON TILDA'S ROOF the next morning. A perfect day for toasted buttermilk biscuits with strawberry jam, she thought. It was the first meal Aunt Sippy had made for her, just after her parents clicked the door shut behind them.

"Everything seems better after you eat a toasted buttermilk biscuit, especially with strawberry jam," her aunt claimed.

And she was right. Young Tilda discovered this with the first bite. The sweetness woke up her taste buds and she felt oddly comforted.

While Tilda ate, Aunt Sippy settled across the table. She wore her long silver hair in two tight braids, and even though she was old, she had freckles sprinkled across her nose.

"Tell me about your gift," Aunt Sippy said.

"Gift?" Tilda had not brought a gift for Aunt Sippy. She wished she had a big box with a red bow and something special inside it for her.

"I'm sorry," Tilda had said. "I didn't bring a gift."

"Nonsense," Aunt Sippy told her. "Everyone has a special gift."

That day Tilda was confused, and while she nibbled her toasted buttermilk biscuit, she wondered if maybe her parents had tucked a gift for Aunt Sippy in her suitcase. But she knew not to bother looking.

Then Aunt Sippy had said, "Maybe you haven't discovered your gift yet. It is up to us to find it, then use it. For a gift should never be wasted."

Tilda thought about that day, so long ago, as she put two leftover biscuits in the oven. She rubbed her hands together, waiting for her breakfast and wondering if she had wasted her gift. A moment later, she opened the front door to fetch the newspaper. Before she could step onto the porch, something tiny scampered inside.

It was *him*! Spider!

"The sky is raining frogs and crickets," Spider said.

All Tilda could think to say was "I need my umbrella."

"A fine howdy-do is that, Miss Butter," said Spider. "Don't you have some tea?"

"Tea?"

"Earl Grey, orange pekoe, even a drop of jasmine would do." Then he softened his voice. "Please, my kind friend."

"You drink tea?" Tilda had forgotten about the newspaper and the rain. She didn't know much about Spider. She didn't much care to know. He had a way of getting on her nerves every time she ran into his webs around her garden. He was a bit pretentious, bragging about his "fine spinning talent." Spider hadn't ever stepped inside her home because she had never invited him in.

"I drink tea every morning," Spider said. "If I can manage."

She hadn't invited him in this morning either. But Tilda went to her cupboard and pulled out a teacup and saucer, her very best, just as she did whenever she had company.

"My goodness gracious, ma'am," Spider said. "Do you want me to drown? Don't you have a thimble?"

Tilda's fingers began to prickle. That prickle traveled up her arm and all the way to her face. She was not used to her morning routine being interrupted, especially by Spider. Why couldn't Isadora have visited instead? She loved hearing about the snake's adventures. She was so sneaky, sliding in and out of every yard on the street. She knew everything about everyone on While-a-Way Lane.

Tilda cleared her throat. "Now, see here, tiny gentleman, you are in *my* house. And—"

"And a very fine house it is, Miss Butter," said Spider, using a sugary tone. "Why, look at those curtains framing your kitchen window. Did you happen to get the lovely silk from that little shop around the corner? If so, I'll have you know, I am acquainted with the McCalaster brothers. They have an excellent reputation. Yes indeed, if you are going to be a silkworm, you'd want to be a McCalaster."

"Well, I—" Tilda didn't know what to say next. She just wished she could remember how to get rid of an unwanted guest so she could fetch her newspaper, drink her mug of tea alone, and devour her buttermilk biscuits.

Unfortunately, Spider knew what to say. "You keep

such an immaculate house, not a speck of dirt, not one crumb."

Tilda knew it wasn't so. Her sink was filled with last night's dishes, her shoes were scattered about, and her entire house needed a good dusting and sweep up. If it weren't for Fred, her floor would be covered with crumbs.

"No ants," continued Spider, who was swinging his front legs in motion across the room and heading toward her table.

"No," Tilda said, "no ants. Just one little spider."

"I always wanted to be bigger, but it's not in my DNA. I think I interrupted you. You were looking for your thimble."

"Was I?" Tilda asked.

"Yes," said Spider. He was on the table now. "You certainly were. But only after you put the kettle on the stove."

Tilda didn't move one inch. She had to figure out this unwanted-guest situation. Where was Fred when she needed him? It didn't matter. Fred would be of no use at scaring Spider away. The only time he barked was when he saw the mailman, Dewey Wonder. No, Fred would be of no help at all. If only she could communicate with him like she did with almost every other creature on While-a-Way Lane. A gift with such a strange exception. What use was her gift, anyway?

Spider was the last creature she would have chosen to speak with. How was she going to get rid of him?

Then a solution came to her. It was so easy, she was surprised she hadn't thought of it before. A guest comes to your house for something. You give it to them. They leave.

"Earl Grey or jasmine?" she asked, filling the kettle with water.

Spider tapped four of his legs on the table. "Let's see. Decisions, decisions. If I have the Earl Grey, I'll be set for the day. Just the right zing to spin and spin. But jasmine sounds so romantic."

When it appeared Spider would never make up his mind, Tilda said, "I'm the classic sort. I'd go with the Earl Grey."

Spider examined Tilda from head to toe. "Yes! Good point. Jasmine it is."

While the kettle perked, Tilda went to her sewing box and found a thimble. When she returned to the kitchen, Spider didn't seem to be anywhere in sight. She looked out the window. The hard rain had turned into a light drizzle. Maybe the rude fellow had decided to leave. Tilda let out a big long sigh. Now she could get on with her day—read the paper, drink her tea, eat her buttermilk biscuits, and go into the garden to dust her hosta.

The kettle whistled.

"Yoo-hoo, Miss Butter?"

Spider was perched on the table in the same spot where Tilda usually placed her biscuits. The very spot.

"Your kettle is call-ing to you," sang Spider. "Call-ing to y-ou."

Tilda marched to the stove and poured the hot water over a bag of jasmine tea. She tapped her foot and waited.

"How about that weather?" Spider was in no hurry.

Tilda drummed her fingers on the countertop.

"Did I mention you have the most exquisite hosta?"

Tilda turned around. "What about my hosta?"

"I saw a grasshopper eyeing those tender leaves, and I quickly spun a web. It was some of my finest work, if I do say so myself. It was sheer and tightly woven. The grasshopper had no idea what he was in for when he hopped my way.

"Such a struggle, he wiggled and squirmed, but it was no use. He lost his fight. Yes indeed, it was a mutually satisfying event."

"How so?" Tilda was thinking of the grasshopper.

"You got to keep your perfect hosta and I got a nutritious meal. One must eat one's greens."

Tilda felt conflicted. She loved her hosta. She had big plans for it, and appreciated Spider's help, but she really wished he would leave.

"You know," said Spider, "I'm like a captain and my web is like a ship. We're constantly on the move and my courage is forever challenged."

Tilda ignored him.

"Mmm, the tea, dear lady?"

Tilda scooped a teaspoon of tea from her cup and dripped it into the thimble. Then she slid it across the table until the thimble reached her guest.

Spider crept up the side of the thimble, and with every move (eight—one for each leg) he yelled, "Hot, hot, hot, hot, hot, hot, hot, hot! I dread this part, but it's so worth it."

Tilda smelled something. The biscuits!

She grabbed a pot holder, quickly opened the oven door, and pulled out the pan. "Almost burned!"

"Oh, they look just perfect," Spider said.

Tilda ignored him, easing the biscuits onto her plate.

"Exactly the way I desire them," continued Spider. "Cocoa-colored like a brown praying mantis."

"Would you have one?" she asked. Aunt Sippy had taught Tilda manners.

"Perhaps just a crumb," he said.

She broke off a tiny bit of biscuit and offered the crumb to Spider.

He accepted it.

Then she noticed his legs shaking like threads on a tassel blowing in the wind.

He pointed with one of them over Tilda's shoulders and squeaked, "Eeee, eee, eee!"

Tilda looked behind her. Fred was coming toward them, probably to give the floor under the table a good sniff in hopes of finding a buttermilk biscuit crumb.

"Sorry to drink and run," Spider said in a breathless voice, "but I have a busy, busy day ahead of me." He spun a thread from the back of the chair and lowered himself down to the floor, taking his crumb with him.

Tilda opened the door, and Spider left the same way he entered. But not before saying, "Good day, Tilda Butter! Thank you for the tea."

Tilda waited until Spider was out of sight. Then she fetched her wet paper, placed a buttermilk biscuit on a plate, and gave Fred's head a nice pat.

"Good boy, Freddie," Tilda said. "You scare spiders after all."

CHAPTER SIX

THE GIANT

THE NEW HOUSE had boxes everywhere. Some were stacked so tall they reminded Daniel of the downtown skyline he could see from his old bedroom window. Pretending he was a giant, he climbed to the top of a pile, making his way to the one that towered above the rest in the center of the room. The one with the box at the top and the words ~~WEDDING~~ CHINA spelled out in black.

Daniel stepped up, up, up. There he was, atop the

highest stack, his head skimming the ceiling. He was taller than anyone in the entire world. Including his dad. Well, not his dad. His dad was the tallest, strongest, smartest person in the whole wide world. If only his dad were here to see him now. Daniel, the giant. He peered down and saw a spider making his way between the boxes. The spider had ahold of something. It looked like a crumb.

If Daniel had had his slingshot, he would have gotten rid of that spider. But he didn't need the slingshot. He was a giant. He could just land on him.

He started to jump to the floor.

Then he decided maybe he shouldn't.

Then he thought, *What the heck.* He swung his arms back, paused, and thought, *Nope. Maybe not.*

With all his shuffling and moving, the china box was inching off the one beneath it. Finally, it slid completely away and hit the floor with Daniel falling on top.

He knew the sound of breaking dishes. He was a champion accidental dish breaker. But this was his mother's ~~WEDDING~~ CHINA. And even though they never once used a piece, even though the china had been stored in a cabinet in the dining room (a room they never used), he knew he was in trouble. He froze, expecting his mother to burst into the room.

Where was she?

The spider, carrying the crumb like a precious jewel, took off from near a box and headed out of the room.

Daniel studied the city of boxes, planning his escape. Slowly, he weaved through the maze of cardboard until he reached the front door. It was raining outside, but he didn't care. Off he ran, racing past the yellow cottage, then the green one, the purple one, and all the others. His sneakers smacked the street, making loud thumps through the raindrops. He didn't stop until he reached the end of the street. He would have kept on, but he couldn't because of what was in front of him.

Daniel had run into a pond.

CHAPTER SEVEN

SNAIL TALE

THE NEXT MORNING the sun shined so brightly every puddle along While-a-Way Lane had disappeared. It was garbage day. From her front window, Tilda saw the woman next door carry a moving box to the curb. Even from where Tilda stood, she could make out the writing on the box. ~~WEDDING~~ CHINA.

Goodness pudding, thought Tilda. No wonder they seemed so sad.

Soon she'd go over with a pie and make introductions. Surely they'd almost finished unpacking.

For now, Tilda would check on her hosta. It was only mid-spring and already the plant measured three feet high and four feet wide. Finally she would have a specimen grand enough to enter in the Falling Star Valley Garden Show.

She could just imagine her hosta, its lime-colored leaves shiny from a careful dusting. And if her entry won first place, it would be included on the Garden Club float in the Falling Star Valley Parade. And best of all, she would get to ride on the float too. She would wave at all of her neighbors as the float made its way down their street. And they would wave back. She'd wanted to be in a parade ever since she was a little girl.

Aunt Sippy always won first place at the garden show. It didn't matter if Aunt Sippy entered a rose or Shasta daisies or hostas. Aunt Sippy could grow anything. Sometimes she dug plants out of dumpsters that neighbors had thrown out because they thought they were dead. Mere days later, they would be thriving under Aunt Sippy's care, growing to gigantic proportions.

While some neighbors' sunflowers peeked over fences, Aunt Sippy's stretched past chimneys, heading to the clouds. Her pumpkins grew so huge, she hollowed out one and made a playhouse for Tilda, complete with cabbage cushions and acorn bowls.

That was Aunt Sippy's gift. Tilda wanted to be like her aunt more than anyone. If only she could win first place at the garden show. Every year she entered, but she never got first, second, or third place. Even an honorable mention would have been dandy.

She could hardly wait to see how much the hosta had grown since she checked it yesterday.

Tilda hurried outside and headed to the garden. There she let out a scream. Holes dotted an entire leaf of her prized plant.

"Please don't shout," said a teeny-tiny voice.

Tilda looked around, but the voice was coming from below. It was coming from her hosta. She lifted the damaged leaf, and there was a teeny-tiny snail peering up at her. She felt the blood leave her face. All she could say was "You! You snail!"

Tilda plucked up the creature and held it with her thumb and forefinger.

The snail's antennas quivered. "Please don't squish me like you did my momma and poppa!"

That was exactly what Tilda had planned to do. But now she asked, "I squished your momma and poppa?"

The snail's antennas nodded. "Over in the arugula patch."

"Those were *your parents?*"

Fred came over to her and rolled on his back. He always did that when he wanted a good tummy scratch.

"Not now, Fred."

But Fred stayed belly side up.

Seemed like time stood still out there in the backyard. Still as a dragonfly resting on a twig, the three of them waiting. Tilda was waiting to figure out what to do with the snail. The snail was waiting to see what Tilda would do with her. Fred was waiting for a scratch.

She gazed at her poor hosta. She studied the snail. It was only a snail. What was one less snail in the world?

Then she remembered. This would be three less snails in the world if you counted this little snail's parents.

"Please, ma'am!" begged the snail.

Tilda straightened her back. "Why did you have to eat my hosta?"

"I'm a snail," the tiny voice said, as if that should make all the sense in the world.

Tilda could feel the smooth surface of the shell between her fingers. This was someone's home.

"If only you'd chewed my arugula." Then she covered her mouth with her other hand because she realized she'd said the dreadful word. *Arugula.*

"But I couldn't bear to go over there." The snail lowered her antennas. "The sadness."

Tilda should never have mentioned the arugula. Still, she had a dilemma. "What am I to do with you, then? If I let you go, you will eat something else in my garden. I had big plans for this hosta. I was going to show it at the Falling Star Valley Garden Show.

"I only nibbled one leaf. You could remove it."

Tilda frowned. "It will be lopsided!"

"If you remove the one across from it, the plant would be even."

Tilda rubbed her chin and imagined the hosta minus two leaves. It was an option, a not so bad one. The hosta would have a couple of leaves missing, but no one would know (not even a garden show judge) because the plant would be perfectly balanced.

"But then what?" Tilda asked. "What am I to do with you?"

"Well," the teeny-tiny snail said carefully, "I've always wanted to be a pet."

"A pet? What in the world would I do with a pet snail?"

"Do you have a terrarium?" asked the snail.

"No," Tilda said. She babied her outdoor plants, but she forgot to water the indoor ones.

"Everyone should have a terrarium," the snail said. "They're no trouble at all. Just imagine, a little garden inside a jar."

Tilda tried to see it. One more thing to dust.

"I'll keep the glass clean," the snail said as if she'd read Tilda's mind.

"And how does such an itsy-bitsy creature as yourself know anything about terrariums?"

"My mother was a terrarium snail until the gentleman who owned it moved away. Before he left, he let Momma loose in the woods. That's where she met my poppa. It was love at first slime. They were so happy until . . . until the . . . arugula patch."

When the teeny-tiny snail started to sniffle, Tilda found herself wondering where she could buy a terrarium. She wondered about that so deeply that without knowing it, she began to scratch Fred's belly. He had fallen asleep on his back, while patiently waiting.

That was how Tilda Butter became a terrarium owner and got a pet who was nothing like her beloved Fred, nothing like him at all.

CHAPTER EIGHT

TOP-NOTCH SPY

ALTHOUGH HIS MOTHER never mentioned the broken china, Daniel found the pieces the next day in the box next to the garbage can—chips with purple flowers from teacups, plates, and bowls. Even the pieces that weren't broken were there.

They'd lived on While-a-Way Lane two whole days and Daniel hadn't seen any kids his age. Not one kid any age. His mom reminded him that it was spring break and that the other kids were probably traveling. Spring break was no fun when everyone else was on vacation. Everyone but the old people.

The only friends he'd met were two squirrels outside his window the first morning he woke up in his new bedroom. The next morning he left peanuts in the yard for them. He was delighted when they came back, but that was the most excitement he'd had since he moved here. Mostly he'd been bored until his dad called each night.

Daniel's mom said she would ride bikes with him when she had a spare moment, but that would be no fun. In his old neighborhood, she had pedaled so slowly because she enjoyed looking at everything. Now she'd probably be twice as pokey since everything would be new here. He thought about going to the pond, but he wanted to wait until his dad could go with him. Then a bigger, better idea came to him. Every street should have a top-notch spy, and While-a-Way Lane's should be him.

Daniel, Top-Notch Spy. He loved the sound of it

so much that he wrote his new title out on a piece of paper and taped it to his bedroom door. His mother would probably never notice anyway. She was too busy looking for a job.

Daniel went outside to start on *his* new job. He was about to begin with the next-door neighbor, the woman he saw talking to herself with the big dog. Then the mail jeep came down the road. He hid behind the bush near his front door, waiting for the vehicle to stop. When it reached his box, Daniel watched a bald man with a round face open it and slip in some envelopes. For a split second he wondered if his dad had written to him. Sometimes his dad sent him postcards from his business trips. Daniel could check later. Right now he was on a mission.

Who was the mailman? Maybe he wasn't a mailman. Maybe he was a spy, too. After all, he saw everyone's mail before they did, didn't he?

When the mailman drove to the house next door, Daniel followed, hiding behind his neighbor's big pot of flowers. Suddenly he heard a dog barking. Had he been discovered? No. The next-door lady's dog was barking at the mailman. Daniel's dad said dogs were good judges of character. He told Daniel their sense of smell was so strong, they knew when someone might be good or bad.

The dog kept barking.

"Stop that, Fred!" It was the lady.

She waved at the mailman. "Hello, Dewey Wonder! Thank you for the mail!"

The mailman waved and drove to the next house. When the lady and the dog disappeared inside her home, Daniel took off down the street, following Dewey Wonder's mail jeep. When Dewey reached the next house, Daniel crossed the road and ducked behind a thick tree trunk.

This time after Dewey Wonder stopped, he got out of the jeep with a small package. Daniel watched Dewey's every move—the way he paced quickly up the walk, the way he glanced down at the faded hopscotch game someone had chalked on the sidewalk, the way he carefully laid the package down on the welcome mat, first taking his handkerchief out and giving it a quick dusting.

"He doesn't fool me," Daniel muttered. Maybe the mailman was about to do something sneaky.

And Dewey Wonder did. On the way back to his jeep, he stopped in front of the chalk lines on the sidewalk, looked both ways, and hopped, hopped, hopped. When he came to the two side-by-side squares, he landed on them with both feet, scissor-crossed his legs two times, then moved forward on one foot. He seemed so pleased with himself that when he reached the top square, he turned around and hopped all the way back.

A hopscotching mailman may have seemed unusual to a boy like Daniel, but he was not looking close enough. If he'd been looking close enough, he would have seen a glimmer of the boy that Dewey Wonder had never let go of.

Young Dewey grew up in a fun-loving, game-playing family. His parents and his competitive little brother, Charlie, played hopscotch, ran relay races (Charlie always won), and did family Hula-Hooping sessions. (Dewey had marvelous balance and could go for hours keeping a Hula-Hoop swirling around his plump waist.)

The Wonders lived at the tip-top of Pointy Mountain, the very one that Daniel could see from his bedroom window. Dewey's family had never visited Falling Star Valley, and so one day they set out to do just that. Their little car wound its way down the mountain, each switchback opening them up to new sights—the cotton balls the Wonders had seen below, they now clearly realized were sheep on a farm, the colorful blocks lined up were cottages on a street, the little puddle was actually a pond.

When they turned on While-a-Way Lane, with the multicolored cottages, Dewey's mother said, "Oh my, these homes are as scrumptious as sherbert."

"Yes, indeed," his father said.

They came to a yellow cottage with sunflowers that towered above the roofline, and Dewey noticed a girl wearing a polka-dotted dress. She was sitting on the lawn, peering between the grass blades. Dewey was in awe, not of the street with the strawberry, lemon, and blueberry hued cottages, nor the giant sunflowers, but of the girl. She was the most beautiful girl he'd ever seen.

Charlie was looking at her too, but he said, "Ehh, it's just a girl."

They made their way down the street to get a closer view of the pond, and they came to a blue cottage with a FOR SALE sign.

"We should move here," his mother said.

Before his father could comment, Dewey blurted, "Yes, we should!"

And they did.

Dewey thought everything on While-a-Way Lane was wonderful, especially Tilda Butter.

Charlie couldn't wait to leave the valley, and when

he grew up, he spun a globe, closed his eyes, put his finger on a spot, and moved there. Have you ever been to Timbuktu? Charlie started an overnight delivery service and lives life at such a fast pace, he's never made time to return to While-a-Way Lane.

Dewey never left. He enjoyed the slower pace his job offered, placing letters in the mailbox that he hoped brought good news. He adored reading the backs of postcards.

What? you ask. *How dare he?*

But Dewey didn't feel a bit guilty about it. He believed a postcard was an invitation to be read. That was how he knew so much about the young boy who moved with his mother into the cottage next to Tilda's.

The boy's father was not living with him and his mother. From what Dewey gathered from the postcard, he wouldn't be. The postcard came from the other side of the county, but he said he'd be traveling to Tokyo and Paris again soon. The man must live out of his suitcase. Dewey knew he missed the boy and had given him a boat that they were going to sail on the pond when he visited. Soon, the man wrote, "Soon." Dewey knew all of this, but he didn't know the boy's name because his father addressed the postcard to the Champ.

Dewey wondered what the boy's real name was and if he'd see him at the pond, sailing his boat.

DANIEL'S FOCUS ON THE MAILMAN was interrupted by a screeching voice behind him.

"Hi, young man! Are you my new student?"

Daniel swung around to find a very old lady staring at him. She was standing with her palms out, stretching and wiggling her long fingers toward the sky. He could see the calluses on the tips.

"Are you my new piano student?" she demanded.

Piano? He would hate playing the piano. Sometimes Daniel's buddy from the old neighborhood couldn't come out to play because his mother made him practice the piano for two hours every day.

"Well?" The old lady's beady eyes peered at him from over glasses that rested low on her hook nose.

She reminded Daniel of a witch.

She tapped her fingertips together as if she were waiting for his answer.

The only thing Daniel could think of saying was "Nope."

Then he raced off, heading for the pink cottage. And a moment later when he reached the front door and went inside, it was the first time he was happy to be there.

CHAPTER NINE

AGATHA BROWN

IF DANIEL HAD LOOKED CLOSER, he would have realized Agatha Brown was not anything like a witch. He would have seen the wistful longing for a different life. Agatha was a frustrated would-be saxophone player.

When she was a young girl, her parents had made her take piano lessons and practice hours on end, just like she demanded of her students. They wanted a child prodigy, but she wasn't a gifted piano player. No doubt, she was good (all that practice!), but she didn't have the heart for the ivory keys. She could hardly wait until bedtime, when she would hide under the sheets and pretend to play the instrument of her dreams.

Every year, on her birthday, she wished the same wish before blowing out her candles. *Please may I be a saxophone player?*

When the flames disappeared, one of her parents always said, "I'll bet you wished for a grand piano."

How could she tell them her real wish? They'd be so disappointed.

One day, on the way home from school, she noticed a path through the woods that bordered the backyards of While-a-Way Lane. She'd never seen the trail before. It was beckoning to her. So she left the street and stepped onto the trail. It was not a straight path, but one that wove around tree trunks and under low branches. She followed it obediently, for she was an obedient child. At the edge of the woods, something dropped and landed with a thump at her feet. When she realized what it was, her heart sprinted a few beats. It was a saxophone! She looked up at the opening between the thick branches, but all she saw were clouds drifting. It was as if the sky had opened up and given her a gift. She decided it was a sign. She scooped up the saxophone, hid it under her coat, and took it home.

Agatha didn't tell her parents for fear that they might take the instrument from her, but every night when young Agatha went to bed, she took out the saxophone, which she'd hidden in her closet, got under the sheets and blanket, and pretended to play just like she did before. But this time her fingers pushed real keys and her lips pursed over a real mouthpiece, being very careful not to blow.

Both of her parents' last words to her had been "Don't forget to practice the piano *every day*." So even though she was a grown-up, after her parents left this world, the most she could bring herself to do was to put on some jazz albums and pretend to play along with the music.

Agatha Brown's parents' dying request hung over her like a dark, brooding cloud. What would happen if she accidentally blew into the mouthpiece? Agatha Brown planned to never know.

CHAPTER TEN

NEIGHBORS

*T*IME TO MEET *the next-door neighbors,* thought Tilda. They had lived on While-a-Way Lane three days now. She pulled out a pan and gathered all the ingredients to make a sugar cream pie. Then she heard a door slam next door.

She glanced out the front window and saw the new neighbor boy stomp from his home. He marched over to the mulberry tree and gave it a big kick. *Perhaps,* she thought, *this is not a good time to meet them.* She would wait another day or two, long enough for their house to get in order.

Instead she slipped on her orange rubber clogs and went outside to pull weeds from the butterfly garden. Fred plodded behind her to find a place to do his business. Seemed these days that was the only reason Fred wanted to go outside.

Ever since Snail became a pet, Fred had stopped looking for Tilda's lap or rolling over, wanting his tummy scratched. From morning on, he watched Snail glide up and down the terrarium. Up, up, up, up and down, down, down, down.

Tilda almost felt jealous. Almost. At least this way she could do a little weeding without having to stop and scratch.

Snail was not shy about asking for extra helpings. The first time Tilda dropped a fat lettuce leaf in the terrarium, Snail looked up and said, "More please."

While Fred sniffed around for a spot, Tilda scanned her garden. Two of her yellow irises were blooming near the big rock. This made her smile. Irises blooming meant the ice cream man would soon be making his rounds on While-a-Way Lane. It meant the lemonade stand would be open after school every day and the Falling Star Valley Garden Show and Parade were just around the corner.

Fred whimpered by the back door and Tilda let him in. Then she returned to the garden, knelt, and pulled the sticky-nicky weeds that had popped up in the butterfly garden. In no time at all, she'd filled her bucket. But she decided to squeeze in one last handful. She grabbed hold of some sticky-nicky and yanked.

Just as she threw it into the bucket, she heard, "Well, excus*sse* me!"

She stared at the bucket. "Hello?" she whispered to the sticky-nicky weeds.

Something moved.

She looked closer.

Two black eyes under the weeds stared up.

Tilda scooted back, but lost her balance and landed sprawled out on the grass with her arms and legs pointed in different directions. She felt like a pretzel. She raised her head.

The snake poked her head out of the bucket.

"It'ssss jussst me, dear lady," said the smooth silky voice.

Tilda sighed. "Oh, Isadora! It *is* you!"

Isadora was a green grass snake. Most lived only a dozen years or so, but Isadora was as old as Tilda. This was, after all, While-a-Way Lane. Do you need to be reminded that things are not as ordinary as they first appear?

Young Tilda had met Isadora when she was digging in her garden. Aunt Sippy had given over a portion of her flower garden for Tilda to plant as she pleased. At first she was ecstatic about having her very own garden, but then she became overwhelmed by the choices. And when she studied Aunt Sippy's garden of cloud-skimming sunflowers and zinnias big enough to be giant powder puffs, her hopes sank as low as shells on an ocean floor. She pulled her hand rake through the dirt until it met the grass. Over and over again, as if the answer would pop out of nowhere.

"How about daissssiessss?" a voice from below her asked.

She squinted her eyes at the grass. Was the grass talking to her?

"Or maybe cosssmosss? They have a lovely airy way about them."

When she finally realized it was a snake talking to her, she almost screamed. She opened her mouth to do just that, but the snake said, "I'm nothing to be afraid of. My name isss Isssadora."

And that was the beginning of a friendship that had lasted through the years.

Isadora was not of the poisonous sort, but Tilda had to remind herself of that because she didn't care for most snakes. She'd avoided them like the dishes that piled up in her sink.

"I forgot you were afraid of sssnakesss!" Isadora said with a sigh. "That'sss why mossst of my friendsss have other namesss now. The word sssnake hasss become sssuch an insssult."

Tilda swallowed and surveyed the grass. "Are your friends here now?"

"They're here, there, over yonder," Isadora said.

"Oh, dear." Tilda stood at once. And when she did, she felt a sharp pain travel up her leg to her hip. "Ouch!" Had one of Isadora's friends bitten her?

"Oops, sorry! I missed." It was the boy next door. He was sitting on the fence with his slingshot.

Now Tilda realized she'd been popped with a pebble.

"I almost got that snake," he said, holding up his weapon. "Were you talking to it?"

Tilda looked to the spot where Isadora had been. Her friend had already slid away.

The boy jumped and landed facedown into her patch of petunias.

Tilda started toward him. "Are you all right?"

The boy bounced up quickly. "I'm fine. Were you talking to that snake?" he asked again.

"Talking to a snake?"

"You were talking to someone," he said. "I heard you."

"Young man, you need to stop using that slingshot. I have a mind to tell your mother." Tilda rubbed her sore spot.

"My mom doesn't care."

"Surely she does," Tilda said, but she was afraid the boy could be right. After seeing the china box with the word *wedding* crossed out, she figured his mother might have a heavy heart these days. And that could keep her mind elsewhere.

She sized the boy up and down. Though he was not a little boy, he was not a big one either. No matter what, he had no business with a slingshot.

"Haven't you met someone nice to play with?" she asked him.

"Nope."

Then Tilda remembered it was spring break. Every young family on the street was away. "A book to read perhaps?"

"Nope."

"A game to play? I wouldn't mind a quick game of checkers." When she was a girl, Tilda had loved playing checkers with her aunt Sippy.

"No one to play with," he said. "No book to read

(except *Peter Pan*—he loved that book), and I don't like checkers anyway."

"Have you ever played checkers?"

"Nope."

Just as she suspected. Tilda looked at the bucket and then the boy.

"See that little hill in the corner of my yard?"

"The garbage?"

"It's my compost pile. All of that trash will become rich and dark one day. Then I'll put it back in the garden."

"Yep," he said. "I see it."

"Could you please help me? Please take this bucket and deposit its contents there."

The boy shoved his slingshot in his back pocket, picked up the bucket, and headed toward the compost pile. He seemed content to do it. Unfortunately, he decided to dump the bucket of vegetable scraps a few feet away from the spot.

"Why did you put it there?" Tilda asked when he returned.

"Two hills are better than one," the boy said.

When he gave the bucket back to her, he asked, "Now what do you want me to do? Kill some snakes? I could stomp on them."

He stomped his feet.

"I could pop them in the head with a rock."

He snapped his slingshot.

"No, thank you," Tilda said. "Let's leave the snakes alone. If we don't bother them, they won't bother us. Besides, some snakes are good. They eat nasty pests."

"Like people?" he asked. His eyes grew as big as the brown centers of sunflowers.

"I don't know," Tilda said. "Are you a pest?"

"Nope."

"Then I guess you don't have anything to worry about."

The boy moved in closer and grabbed Tilda's trowel. "Do you want me to dig up something for you?"

"No, that's quite all right."

He dropped the trowel, ran, and hopped onto the big rock in the iris bed. "I can do a lot of things."

The boy jumped and landed in the middle of the irises, crushing two sunny blooms.

"Careful, young man!"

"Sorry," he said, trying to straighten the broken stems. "But you have lots of them."

"But now I have two less."

He turned away from her, and his eyes searched the entire yard, like he was trying to find something else to talk about. "You have a whole bunch of flowers." He started toward the big oak. "Hey, what is that squatty green thing around the tree?"

"A hosta," she said. *Please stay away from it,* she almost added, but changed her mind. This boy seemed the type who would be tempted to destroy something if it were forbidden.

It occurred to Tilda that she didn't know the boy's name. "If we're going to talk about snakes and plants, we should at least introduce ourselves. I'm Tilda Butter."

"That's a funny name," the boy said.

She waited for the boy to introduce himself, but he

just glanced around Tilda's yard like he was planning his next adventure.

"What's your name?" Tilda asked cheerfully.

"Can't tell you."

"Oh?"

"Nope, you're a stranger. I'm not supposed to tell strangers my name or where I live."

"That's very good advice," Tilda said.

"How old are you?" he asked, sizing her up and down.

Tilda frowned. Though she was not an old woman, she was not a young one either. "Didn't your mom say anything about talking to strangers?"

"Nope."

"Are you sure about that?"

"Not sure, and I can't be blamed for things I don't know about."

Tilda studied her two broken irises that now looked like two ladies dressed in yellow who had fainted.

"Well," the boy said, "how old are you?"

"Older than you and younger than that tree." Tilda was pointing to the ancient oak.

"How old is that tree?"

Tilda could see the conversation was going to last a lot longer than she wanted.

"Excuse me, young man, but I've some things to do inside."

"What kind of things?" he asked.

"Oh, a book to read and maybe a game of checkers."

"Okay." He tucked his slingshot into his back pocket. "I'll come again tomorrow in case you have a bucket for me to empty or some snakes to kill."

Tilda left the boy in her garden. Once inside, she watched him from between the curtains. He had not left yet. Instead he was trying to stake the irises with some kind of green string tied to sticks.

"There is good in everyone," Tilda said. Then she realized the green was not string at all, but her sweet pea vine that had been due to bloom any day now.

CHAPTER ELEVEN

MOONLIGHT RIDE

Daniel's mother had a new job. She would be gone before he left for school and wouldn't be home until dinnertime. Now Daniel wore a front-door key on a chain around his neck. His shirt would hide the key, but his mom said it would be next to his heart and that he'd know she was thinking of him even when she wasn't at home. When she said that, Daniel wanted to say he wouldn't have to wear the stupid key if they were still with his dad.

To celebrate her new job, Daniel's mom said they could go out to a restaurant and eat, but when he suggested Macaroni Joe's, she asked him to pick another place. She said it was too far, but he knew the real reason. She just didn't want to go anywhere his dad had been with them. They used to go to Macaroni Joe's anytime they celebrated anything—his dad's promotion, or Daniel's good report card, or even the first snow of the year. Nothing would ever be the same.

He and his mom had lived on While-a-Way Lane five days. This Sunday would be the last day of spring break, and Monday he'd have to go to his new school. He missed his old school, his home, his friends, and his dad. The day after they moved in, his dad called him and said that he'd visit in a couple of days, as soon as he finished his big project.

But his dad hadn't visited. Maybe it was because his mom wouldn't be happy if he did. It didn't seem too long ago that the three of them had gone on a hike in the forest and fed torn pieces of leftover bread to the birds.

Whenever his dad finally came for a visit, Daniel had

the day all planned. He would show his dad the pond, and they could sail the boat there. He'd introduce him to his new friends—the two squirrels that ate the peanuts he dropped in the yard each morning outside his bedroom window.

The other day, he slept later than usual and he awoke to their chattering on his windowsill. He hurried outside and threw the peanuts on the ground. Then he backed away five long steps and watched them eat. Once they finished, they scampered off to the big oak in Tilda Butter's yard. Each day he planned to move in a few inches closer after he dropped the peanuts. Soon he would eat his oatmeal next to them while they ate their breakfast.

Since the other kids that lived on the street hadn't returned yet, he explored While-a-Way Lane by himself. He would show his dad everything, including the secret pathway he'd created weaving through the neighborhood. He knew where every loose picket was in every fence and he'd found out that thick hedges made the best hiding places.

After all, he was Daniel, top-notch spy. He especially loved spying on Tilda Butter, the woman he'd caught talking to a snake. Today he thought he saw her whispering to a bush in the front yard. When she went inside, Daniel rushed over to it and discovered a lizard. But when he said hello to the lizard, all it did was puff out a little red pouch under its throat. That was interesting, but he wished the lizard had talked to him.

That night he rode his bicycle later than he ever had. Clouds covered the moon, and not a star was in sight. It was very dark. Daniel was not scared, though. Well, maybe a little. He pretended his stuffed snail, Snappy, was sharing the seat with him. He sure wished he hadn't given him away.

He rode his bike out of the driveway and pedaled slowly past Tilda Butter's home. Her light was on, and he could see her through the window. She was sitting in a plump chair with a book on her lap. Nearby, her dog was looking at something. When he leaned in closer, he discovered the dog was staring at a terrarium.

Maybe he could knock on Tilda Butter's door, and

she'd ask him inside and make hot cocoa for him. Wasn't that what old ladies did for kids? When he was little, he'd seen a picture of a grandmother, doing that in a storybook. He didn't have a grandmother, and Tilda Butter kind of looked like one.

But he changed his mind. She'd probably tell him it was late and that he needed to go home. If she knew about the china, she'd never ask him over for hot cocoa. Daniel pedaled slowly so he could watch Tilda Butter and her dog as long as possible.

He saw a group of tiny twinkling lights in front of him. Was it a falling star? The sparkles moved closer in and surrounded Daniel, casting a glow on him like a spotlight. Fireflies!

Until now, he'd never seen any, but last year his teacher had read a story about them. The story talked about how kids caught the insects and put them in mason jars with hole-punched lids.

Daniel pedaled quickly past Tilda Butter's mailbox just to see what the fireflies would do. To his amazement, they kept up, circling him like a hug.

Faster, he pedaled faster. The fireflies flew faster. When he reached the mailman's house, he slowed his pace. The fireflies slowed their pace. The mailman had not lowered the shades yet, and Daniel could see him in his pajamas, sitting on a sofa, reading a book (just like Tilda Butter!).

He thought the mailman was wearing a nightcap, but then Daniel realized it was a cat curled up on top of his bald head. Daniel almost laughed, but he kept on down the street all the way to the pond. He and the fireflies.

Then back to the other end of the street. He did it again, except this time he stopped at the edge of the pond. The fireflies flew out a few feet, hovering above the water. Their reflections caused the pond to glisten. Daniel thought they were leaving, and he said, "Goodbye!"

He wished his dad were here to see them. He had started to pedal away when he noticed the fireflies had caught up and were circling him again.

Just as he almost reached his house, he heard his mother calling out his name, but Daniel and the fireflies kept going. He looked toward Tilda Butter's home. Her curtains were now closed. That disappointed him because he'd planned to yell, "Look at me!"

Music came from the piano teacher's house across the street. It didn't sound like piano music. It sounded like a radio inside her house. He slowed his pace to watch a dancing shadow on the upstairs shade. It was the piano teacher. He recognized the hooked nose. She was holding something. It looked like an instrument. A saxophone? But she wasn't playing it. He watched for a second and then picked up his speed.

The third time he passed his house, his mother was yelling his name and starting to count.

The fifth time he passed, she was still counting. She was up to three hundred and seventy-two. She'd never made it to four hundred. She always threatened to punish him if she ever reached that number.

Daniel turned around, peddling toward home.

When he got there, his mother was now up to 399 ⅝. He should have hurried, but instead he straddled the bike and watched the fireflies flutter away.

"Good night!" he told his new friends. "Come back soon!"

CHAPTER TWELVE

DANIEL

THE BOY'S NAME was Daniel. He had not told her, but Tilda had heard his mother calling him from her kitchen window. Seemed his mother was always hollering for him to come in or go out. After meeting him, Tilda understood how a mother might be exhausted if he asked such ongoing questions as he had asked Tilda. They'd lived there a week now. Tilda figured that was enough time for boxes to be emptied and knickknacks dusted and placed in their new spots.

That was why, instead of going into the garden like

on any other spring morning, she went into the kitchen to make a sugar cream pie for Daniel's family.

Tilda hadn't set out to make eight pies, but she had a big carton of cream, and she thought, *Why not?* Baking pies made her happy.

Tilda baking pies made Fred happy, too. She was sure to slosh some of the sweet filling onto the floor, and when she did, Fred would be ready. He considered licking the floor clean his duty.

It was an unspoken agreement this pie-making duo had between them, an agreement that always resulted in a spotless floor and fine pies ready to slice. If only Fred could do the dishes.

While she gathered the ingredients, she felt like she was being watched. And she was. The two squirrel brothers, Zip and Zap, were outside the window, following her every move. Zip and Zap were not her favorite neighbors. They dug up and gobbled down her tulips. They planted acorns all over her yard. They tipped over her wooden statue of Saint Francis. To Tilda, Zip and Zap were pure mischief!

Now she noticed them from the corners of her eyes. They were flicking their tails as she measured the sugar, but when she cracked the eggs, the brothers froze, staring. Then back to flicking their tails again. Until she added the flour. They watched so intently, as if holding their breaths. This happened when she added the cream and vanilla, too.

The moment Tilda slipped two of the pies in the oven, their tails pointed at the ground. They seemed disappointed.

Later, when Tilda finished, she placed the pies in the wagon on her porch and read her list. She'd made a pie for eight of her neighbors.

The sun was shining bright in a cloudless sky. She could see the tip of Pointy Mountain and the top seat of the library's Ferris wheel on the next street. Six houses down the lane, she noticed Dewey Wonder's jeep, moving slow, so slow that Tilda thought Dewey might have fallen asleep at the wheel.

"Beware of s*ss*low-moving objects*ss*," a familiar voice said.

Tilda peered down. It was Isadora, her body stretched up over the patch of daffodils so that she could see the road.

"Dewey Wonder is nothing to beware of," Tilda said. "But I'm curious why he's driving so slowly."

"You don't know?" asked Isadora.

"No," Tilda said, "do you?"

The way Isadora had asked that, Tilda could have sworn she winked, but that would have been impossible since snakes don't have eyelids.

"Well, do you know?" Tilda asked again.

"Oh, I have a hunch he *ssseesss sss*omething inter-e*sss*ting." And with that, Isadora slid away.

Tilda had no idea what she meant. She dismissed Isadora's comment from her thoughts and started toward her wagon, but was stopped in mid-step by Spider dangling from a string of web in front of her. He swung back and forth. Back and forth.

Tilda had to restrain herself from swatting.

Spider groaned. "Oh, I hate this part—beginning!"

"Surely you aren't going to make a web on *my* porch," said Tilda.

"I can't very well live next door," Spider said. "That deplorable child!"

Tilda did not have to ask whom Spider was talking about.

"He tried to squish me!"

"You don't say?" said Tilda.

"But I'm the captain of my ship, looking out to ever-changing views. Courage and persistence come with the territory."

Fred barked.

Dewey had finally stopped in front of her mailbox, and Tilda welcomed the chance to leave Spider. She would deal with him and his web later.

Tilda waved and called out, "Good day, Dewey Wonder! Don't drive off yet. I have a pie for you."

Dewey waited. Even from the porch, Tilda noticed Dewey's face was pink, including the top of his shiny bald head. By the time she dragged her wagon of pies to his jeep, he looked like an apple wearing a mailman's uniform.

"Dewey Wonder, your face is flushed."

Fred growled at Dewey.

"Quit it, Fred," Tilda said. "You know what, Dewey? I'll bet this pie is exactly what you need." She handed the pie over to him.

"Th-thank you," Dewey stammered. "Th-thank you v-very m-much."

Poor man, Tilda thought. She was used to Dewey always sputtering out his words. He'd done that since they were children together, but she'd never seen his face turn as scarlet as her roses.

"Oh, dear, Dewey," Tilda said. "You *are* sick. You better get to the doctor's office as soon as you finish your shift. Then when you go home, have some pie."

Dewey nodded, raised his hand in a small wave, and drove away.

Fred barked until Dewey's jeep was out of sight.

"Goodness pudding, Fred! I don't know why you don't like Dewey Wonder. He's one of the nicest people who live on While-a-Way Lane. And he always delivers the mail on time."

Just as she started to head toward her new neighbors' home, Zip and Zap darted in front of her. And did Fred bother to bark at them? No, indeed. He just sat and watched the squirrel brothers with fascination like he watched Snail.

One of the squirrels (Tilda could not tell them apart) stopped and stuck his nose in the air, sniffing. He moved closer toward Tilda's wagon.

"Are there nuts in that pie?" he asked.

"No, there are not," Tilda said smugly.

"Well, that's a shame," he said.

The other squirrel nodded. "Yes, that's a pity."

"Well," said one of the brothers, "the next time you make a pie, put some nuts in it for Zip."

So this was Zip.

The other squirrel flicked his tail. "No, put some nuts in it for Zap."

"Zip!" said Zip.

"Zap!" said Zap.

Zip began to chase Zap in a circle. It made Tilda dizzy to watch, but Fred followed them so closely his head looked like it could spin off his neck. The whole time they jabbered.

"Zip!"

"Zap!"

"Zip!"

"Zap!"

Fred lowered his body onto the grass. If he could not have a pie, watching squirrels chase each other would have to do.

Tilda moved away from them, pulling her wagon toward her new neighbors' home. "Come on, Fred!"

Fred caught up with Tilda. He didn't want to miss out if a pie fell off the wagon.

When Tilda knocked on the front door, nobody answered, but soon she noticed one eyeball peeking between the curtains.

Daniel spread the curtains wide. Then he cracked open the window. "Whatcha got?"

"Oh," Tilda said. "Hello, there—" She almost spoke

his name, but decided not to since she'd only overheard his mother saying it. "I've made a pie for your family."

"I don't like pie."

"You might like this one. Everyone on While-a-Way Lane likes my pies."

He wrinkled up his nose. "Is it gooey?"

"It's a sugar cream pie, so it's creamy."

"Oh," he said, "it's gooey."

"Is your mom home?"

Daniel frowned. "I can't tell you that."

"Then I'll leave it right here on the porch. Maybe your mom will want a piece of my gooey pie."

"Yeah," he said, "she'll eat anything."

"Very well, good afternoon! Hope you enjoy your first day at Falling Star Valley School."

Tilda turned to go, but Fred hung back, studying the pie on the porch. *Does this count as a dropped pie?*

"Come on, Fred," Tilda said. "We have more deliveries to make."

Fred sulked, following Tilda.

As she headed away from Daniel's house, the door

squeaked open behind her. When she heard it shut, she turned and noticed Daniel through the window. He poked a finger in the middle of the pie and then stuck it in his mouth. His eyes popped wide, and his finger returned for more.

Tilda sighed a deep sigh filled with satisfaction and delight. Her sugar cream pie recipe had not failed her yet.

CHAPTER THIRTEEN

THE RETURN

IT WAS DUSK, that sliver of time caught between day and night. Spring break was coming to an end. From his front yard, Daniel watched car after car and minivan after minivan return to While-a-Way Lane.

Bumper stickers and words spelled out with shaving cream were like banners telling of the neighbors' whereabouts from the last week. SEE THE GRAND CANYON. AMARILLO OR BUST. I ATE TACOS IN SANTA FE. ELVIS IS ALIVE AND WELL IN MEMPHIS.

Daniel thought about hanging a sign on the back of

his bike that read MY PARENTS GOT A DIVORCE AND I HAD TO MOVE TO WHILE-A-WAY LANE.

Even though the neighbors drove in from so many places, they all seemed to arrive at once. One of the drivers honked his horn as he headed down While-a-Way Lane and then the other drivers honked, too. It sounded like a song. Daniel listened closer. It *was* a song. He'd heard it before. "Yankee Doodle"! Everyone waved arms out car windows and honked horns and shouted to each other.

"Hey, neighbor, wait till you hear about the fish I almost caught!"

"Hey, neighbor, I have some pictures to share of our ride on an elephant!"

"Hey, neighbor . . . hey, neighbor . . ." On and on and on.

Tilda Butter stepped out onto her porch and waved at each vehicle as it passed. The piano teacher with the long fingers waved at them, too. Daniel bet she was glad she could torture her students with learning chords and scales again.

The neighbors followed each other like a parade, driving all the way down to the pond and then turning around, honking until their wheels met their driveways.

"Welcome back!" Tilda Butter hollered. "Welcome home!"

They were so happy to be home.

Daniel felt hollow inside. While-a-Way Lane would never be home to him. He didn't want to live here, this place with all these happy people and air that smelled like cotton candy.

Just as he was wishing his dad were with him he saw something sparkle in front of him. It flashed three times. Then there were a hundred flashes. Maybe a thousand. And even though the sun wasn't quite down yet and the moon was nowhere to be found, his friends had returned.

"I knew you'd come back," he told the fireflies. With that, he began to pedal, and together, they made their way down While-a-Way Lane.

CHAPTER FOURTEEN

BIRD FEEDER

TILDA OPENED THE DRAPES to the wide window in the living room, the one that faced her new bird feeder. The bird feeder hung from a low branch of the crape myrtle tree. She wished she could have hung it higher, but Tilda was not very tall, and she didn't much care to step on a ladder. She felt a bit like Fred watching Snail's slow drag, only there was no action this morning. There hadn't been any since she'd hung it a week ago.

Just when she thought of giving up, she saw a branch

move. Could it be the chickadees she loved with their little black hoods? Maybe it was the house finches returning. She loved them, too. Their orange-red faces delighted the bird-watcher in her.

She grabbed her notebook, ready to record any sighting. Then she would promptly notify the Falling Star Valley Bird-Watcher's Society of her keen observations. But it was not a chickadee. It was not a house finch. No, it was Zip and Zap, the squirrel brothers, and they were eyeing the bird feeder like they were trying to size up the jump.

Tilda stood and flapped her arms overhead, but it was too late. Zip and Zap were above the bird feeder. Zip (at least Tilda thought it was Zip) made his way down to the flat part and was riding it belly down like a surfer making his way out in the ocean. The feeder swung. Then Zap landed on top of the feeder, causing it to swing back and forth. Back and forth. Back and forth. They seemed giddy as they munched away at the seed.

Tilda opened the window and hollered, "That is not a squirrel feeder! That is a bird feeder!"

Zip and Zap ignored Tilda. Zip sat up. He'd filled his mouth with so much seed he had chipmunk cheeks.

Tilda shook her fist as he gobbled down thistle and sunflower seed mix.

Zap tried to make his way down, but the feeder was still moving and he jumped so hard that he missed and landed on the ground. Zip and the feeder followed with a big splat.

Fred turned from Snail's terrarium. When he saw the squirrels, he let out a weak "woof."

Zip and Zap didn't stop eating.

Fred gave his attention back to Snail.

Tilda decided she'd waited long enough. She would return the bird feeder today, so she went in the garden to pick it up.

The brothers scampered off when they saw Tilda coming their way. But they left with full bellies.

Outside, the children of While-a-Way Lane were

headed toward school. Tilda stopped and watched. They walked in groups of two, three, or four.

Except for one.

Daniel tagged way behind as if he wanted no part of them. Her heart broke, not just at the sight of him walking all alone, but also because she remembered her own first day at Falling Star Valley School. Everyone had been very nice, but it didn't matter. She felt alone. And when school ended that first day, she felt different, too, as she watched the other children leave the school and run into the arms of their mothers.

Then she had seen someone watching her from across the schoolyard. A woman with two long gray braids hanging beneath her wide straw hat. She wore a soiled apron over her ankle-length skirt and muddy, chunky work boots. Aunt Sippy looked as if she'd stepped away from a hard day in the garden. When she stretched out her arms in little Tilda's direction, Tilda ran to her. Their arms circled each other, and they'd stayed that way for a nice while.

"What a shame," said the grass near her feet.

Tilda gasped but then realized it was Isadora. She wished her friend wouldn't sneak up on her.

"He'*sss ss*such a *sss*ad little fellow when he i*sss*n't annoying."

"Yes, he is," Tilda said. Then she glanced down at the bird feeder. "I'm afraid I can't chat this morning. I have a task to do."

"*Sss*o do I," Isadora said. "I'm *sss*tarved, and I need to get *sss*ome breakfa*ssst*."

Tilda almost asked Isadora if she happened to eat squirrels, but changed her mind. Before she took off for the Fine Feathered Friends Shop, she examined her front porch to make sure Spider had not returned. She was relieved to see no trace of him. Then she took three steps off the porch and heard, "Yoo-hoo, Miss Butter!"

Tilda swung around and looked at the porch once more. She still didn't find him. "Where are you?"

"Over here!" hollered Spider. His voice was coming from the mailbox.

She walked over and opened it.

"Not in there. Underneath!"

Tilda bent low and discovered a sheer veil of web attached to the frame and the bottom of the mailbox.

"Doesn't it make the finest roof?" He sounded so pleased with himself. "No more rainy days for me."

Tilda almost protested, but then she remembered that not-so-long-ago rainy day when she had to share her tea and buttermilk biscuit with him. Maybe he would no longer need to find refuge inside her house.

"How very practical," she said. "Welcome!"

"Thank you, Miss Butter," Spider said. "And now we can get acquainted more often."

"At this moment I must be on my way." With Tilda's parting words, she left for Fine Feathered Friends.

The shop was located on This 'n' That Street, two streets over from While-a-Way Lane. It was between Fly Me to the Moon Kite Shop and Penny's Pogo Stick Store. Even if you had never been there, you couldn't miss it. Fine Feathered Friends had a sign in the shape of a birdcage with a yellow canary painted over each *F*. The peacock-blue front door had a little bell on it that didn't ring, but made a *tweet-tweet* sound when you entered.

The owner, Mr. Oliver, had a long mustache that curled up at each end like the tail of a comma. He wore a straw hat and a red and white striped shirt because he was in a barbershop quartet and he wanted to be prepared in case they had a last-minute call for a fill-in performance. Seemed that was the only time the barbershop quartet ever got booked.

When Tilda stepped inside the store, she was in a very sour mood. She held out the bird feeder to Mr. Oliver. "This is not a bird feeder. It is a squirrel feeder!"

Mr. Oliver didn't bat an eye, which disappointed Tilda. She was so angry about the situation she'd hoped to scare him a little.

But Mr. Oliver smiled and twisted one end of his mustache. "Hmmm," he sang out like he was warming up for a song. "I have just the thing for you."

"I don't want it for me," Tilda said. "I want it for the

chickadees. They are due to arrive this time of year, and they will find other places to nest and eat if squirrels continue to gobble up the seed."

Mr. Oliver presented her with an oblong feeder. It had a little wire grid surrounding it. "This, madam, is a squirrel-proof bird feeder."

He demonstrated it, trying to push his index finger through an opening. "See?" he said. "They can't reach through the grid. But the openings are big enough for tiny beaks."

Tilda raised an eyebrow. "Are you certain about that?" He'd seemed so sure about the last feeder.

"Guaranteed squirrel-proof."

"Or?"

Mr. Oliver looked confused. "Or?"

"Or?" Tilda repeated.

"Oh." Mr. Oliver understood now. "Or your money back."

"Every penny?"

"Every penny."

Tilda tried to wiggle her pinkie finger into the grid, but it was too thick to go through. She wondered about Zip's and Zap's reach. She studied the feeder in silence.

"Tell you what," Mr. Oliver said. "I'll throw in this birdhouse for your trouble."

It was a beautiful birdhouse, white with a little steeple. It looked like the church on the edge of her neighborhood.

"Very well," Tilda said, "I'll give it a try." She really did want to see those chickadees.

When she opened the shop door to leave, Mr. Oliver said once more, "One hundred percent squirrel-proof."

"Or?" Tilda wanted to be reassured.

"Or your money back," Mr. Oliver sang out in a deep baritone voice.

Tilda walked home with the birdhouse in one hand and the 100 percent squirrel-proof feeder in the other. She could just imagine the chickadees nesting there. It reminded her of the days so long ago when Pip-Tweet would show up and lay her eggs in the holly.

It would be entertaining to watch the mother feed

her young and later teach them to fly from the perch. She pictured the little family. The sight of them would make her happy, not like seeing Spider every day. She got so caught up thinking about it, she forgot to stop at Green Things for oranges.

At home, she got the dreaded ladder and hammered a post into the ground and attached the birdhouse. The whole while, she tried not to think about falling by whistling a tune she learned from Aunt Sippy.

Then she filled the feeder and arranged it in the exact spot where she'd hung the last one.

When she finished, she stepped back and admired her work. "There, you pesky squirrels, try that!"

Tilda went back into the house to do some chores, but she had trouble staying focused. She stared out the window at the bird feeder as she washed the dishes, forgetting to dry them before she put them away. Afterward she accidentally ran the vacuum hose over Fred's back instead of the rug. She apologized, but a moment later, she dusted the coffee table with his tail.

Poor Fred! He hid under the bed in fear of what she might do next.

When Tilda finished with her chores, she pushed her chair by the window and plopped down. Waiting.

No one came.

Not the chickadees.

Not the house finches

Not even Zip and Zap.

She grew tired and began to wonder about Daniel's first day at school. Would his mother be waiting for him when school let out?

CHAPTER FIFTEEN

LOST BOY

O N THE WAY TO SCHOOL, Daniel hung way back so that he stayed behind all the other kids. He didn't feel like being the new boy. If they didn't see him, he wouldn't have to be. And it had worked. He was almost at school, and not one person had noticed him.

As soon as he turned the corner onto Wit's End, he froze. The Ferris wheel was working, and there were people in the seats. Not kids, but old people, really old people. Some were laughing, swinging their legs high above his head. A few were reading books, not seeming to notice that they were circling up into the air. One gray-haired man waved down at him. Why were all these old people riding the Ferris wheel?

"It's Senior Day at the library."

He spun around.

A girl with black curly hair smiled at him. It was as if she'd read his mind.

"Aren't you the new boy?" she asked.

"Yep, I guess."

"What's your name?" she asked.

He didn't say the same thing he'd said to Tilda Butter when she'd asked. Instead the words spilled out of his mouth. "The New Boy."

She laughed. "New Boy? I guess that makes me the Lemonade Girl. You better hurry up, New Boy, or you're going to be late for school." She took off sprinting ahead of him.

The Lemonade Girl was right. By the time he reached the front door, the last bell was ringing. His first day at his new school, and he was already tardy. The sign pinned to the bulletin board in the main hall was the reason he hadn't made it to homeroom. He read it again.

WANTED
ONE LOST BOY
For the end of the school year's production of
PETER PAN.
Needed immediately
See Mrs. Garcia

Daniel could hardly breathe. He'd never been in a play, but he'd read the book *Peter Pan* many times. He could be a lost boy. He could be Curly. Curly was his favorite lost boy. He was always getting into trouble. Maybe Daniel could even use his slingshot in the play. To think, he hadn't wanted to come to school today.

He hurried to his homeroom, where his new teacher was taking roll.

The other students were already seated, but Daniel went straight to the teacher and told her, "I have to see Mrs. Garcia immediately. She needs me."

"Oh?" the homeroom teacher said, peering over her glasses. "Aren't you the new boy?"

"I'm the *lost boy* now," Daniel said. "What class is Mrs. Garcia in?"

"Room two twenty-six, but—"

Daniel did not wait until she finished. He took off down the long empty hall, reading the classroom numbers. Two twenty, two twenty-two, two twenty-four. Finally, two twenty-six.

Daniel was so excited, his heart pounded fast in his chest. He swung the door open, stepped inside, and announced, "I'm here! I came immediately!"

The students burst into laughter. Mrs. Garcia's eyebrows touched, and she said the exact thing that his homeroom teacher had said a moment before: "Oh?"

"I'm your lost boy," Daniel said. "But now you found me. Or I guess I found you."

"Ah!" She nodded. "I see."

He spoke fast. "Is the lost boy Curly? I'd be the perfect Curly."

Daniel waited for her to say, *Thank goodness.* Or, *Do you have a slingshot?*

Instead Mrs. Garcia asked, "Can you come back to my class at recess? That's when I'm doing auditions."

Now Daniel softly said, "Oh."

It hadn't occurred to him that anyone else might get the part. The poster seemed to be talking directly to him.

Mrs. Garcia walked him to the door. "Right now you need to return to your homeroom."

That's exactly what Daniel did, but he watched the clock all morning. He watched it as he ate his peanut-butter-and-honey sandwich, not even bothering to read the note his mom wrote on a napkin. He thought about how he'd invite his dad to come see him in the play. And how his dad would think he was the best lost boy. The best Curly.

At recess he went back to Mrs. Garcia's class. She wasn't there, but there were two other boys waiting. They wore matching blue shirts, plaid bow ties, and jeans.

"What are you doing here?" Daniel asked them. Then he realized they looked exactly alike. "Hey, are you twins?"

"Yes," they both said.

"Why do you think we look exactly alike?" asked one of the boys.

"Except for our belly buttons." They said the words together like they'd recited them a zillion times.

"I have an outie," said one.

"And I have an innie," said the other.

Daniel almost asked if they were auditioning, but that couldn't be the reason they were there. There was only one role open for one lost boy, and that part belonged to him.

Before they could tell him why they were there, Mrs. Garcia walked in. She stared at the two other boys, her head turning from side to side. "Oh my goodness! You're identical twins!"

"Except for their belly buttons," Daniel added.

"This is great," Mrs. Garcia said. "I needed another lost boy to replace the lost boy who got strep throat and had to drop out. He was playing the other twin. And now I have real twins! You boys can play the twins."

Daniel straightened his shoulders and stepped forward. He wanted to make sure Mrs. Garcia hadn't forgotten about him. She was so busy smiling at the twins, looking back and forth at them like they'd invented ice cream.

Daniel cleared his throat. "What does the other kid look like? Maybe we could be twins. We might even have matching belly buttons."

Mrs. Garcia turned toward Daniel. "Don't worry. You can be a lost boy, too."

"Curly?" he asked.

She shook her head, but she was still studying the twins. "No, we have a Curly. You will be Lost Boy #8."

"There are only six lost boys," Daniel told her. He was an expert on *Peter Pan*.

"Well, we will have eight," Mrs. Garcia said.

"What happened to #7?" Daniel asked.

She focused on him now. "That will be the boy that was going to play the other twin. See? It all works out."

Daniel didn't see it that way. There were six lost boys in *Peter Pan*. His mother had read it to him when he was too little to read, and now he read it all the time. Well, at least he reread all his favorite parts, the ones with the lost boys, and Captain Hook, and the pirates. Yes, he knew the story well enough to know there were only six lost boys. And none of them were named Lost Boy #8. On top of all that, she didn't let them audition.

Mrs. Garcia handed the twins and Daniel their scripts and the school rehearsal schedule. "The other kids have rehearsed for over a month," she said. "So don't miss any rehearsals. Make sure to tell your parents, too."

When Daniel's mom got off early to pick him up from his first day of school, he didn't give her the schedule. He didn't tell her about getting the role, a made-up role. Maybe he wouldn't tell his dad either.

CHAPTER SIXTEEN
THE ARRIVAL

Tʜᴇ ɴᴇxᴛ ᴍᴏʀɴɪɴɢ, Tilda got up extra early, opened the drapes, stared at the bird feeder, and waited.

She realized she was waiting for Zip and Zap as much as she was waiting for chickadees. Then she saw something. It didn't look like a bird. It didn't look like a squirrel.

Tilda leaned closer to the window. It was a MOUSE!

His long, skinny nose fit through the grid and reached the birdseed.

Tilda raised the window and yelled, "This is not a mouse feeder! This is a bird feeder!"

The mouse, being a mouse, was scared. He took a nosedive into the ferns below . . . *or* did he faint into the ferns? Tilda wasn't so sure. All she knew for certain was that she was taking this feeder back to the Fine Feathered Friends Shop. But just as she was about to move away from the window, she heard a *chicka-dee-dee-dee*. Two chickadees had found the bird feeder and were enjoying a meal so much that some of the seed dropped to the ground, where the little mouse and his two friends began having a feast of their own. Not a bit of seed was going to waste.

"Welcome back, chickadees!" she called out to them.

"Thank you, Tilda Butter," the chickadees tweeted.

"Yes, thank you," squeaked the mice.

"Now, that's as it should be," Tilda said. Then her gaze traveled to the birdhouse, where she now saw Zip, or maybe it was Zap, sticking his head out of the birdhouse's hole. The brothers had found a new home.

CHAPTER SEVENTEEN
FIRST REHEARSAL

THE THIRD DAY OF SCHOOL, Daniel had to stay later for his first rehearsal. When Mrs. Garcia told Daniel to call his mom, he walked down the hall and then turned back to the auditorium. He didn't need to call his mom. She was at work. He'd be home before she would. Besides, he still didn't want her to know about the play.

The entire cast wasn't there because they were rehearsing a scene with the other lost boys and Peter Pan. Mrs. Garcia gave him a cast list.

Daniel looked at the names. A boy named Leonard

was playing Curly. He bet Leonard didn't even own a slingshot. Then he looked at the other cast members' names. Two girls were playing Nana. Mrs. Garcia was terrible at casting. She'd divided the poor dog in half. One girl was playing the front half, and the other was playing the back half.

Nana should be played by a real dog. A big dog. And Daniel knew just where to find one.

CHAPTER EIGHTEEN

ATTIC

Zip and Zap had been Tilda's neighbors for years. Before moving into Tilda's new birdhouse, they lived in the giant oak tree in the back of her yard. (The one that shaded her beloved hosta.) But last night's hailstorm had made such a *ding-ding* racket on the birdhouse's tiny wood roof that when the storm was over, they set out to find better digs.

The storm had dropped one grapefruit-sized hailstone on Tilda's roof, making a very nice opening into the attic. How convenient for the squirrel brothers!

To them, that hole was saying, *Welcome, Zip! Welcome, Zap! Come on in and make yourselves at home!*

That is exactly what they did.

Tilda had no idea about the hole because the hail-stone had landed on a hideous overstuffed chair that once belonged to Tilda's aunt Phoebe. Aunt Phoebe was not Aunt Sippy. Her tight bun reminded Tilda of a burnt cinnamon roll, and her face resembled leather pulled over a drum. If anyone had wanted, they could have bounced pennies off her cheeks. Then at night when she unpinned her hair, every wrinkle returned like a linen shirt pulled straight out of the washer.

Little Tilda dreaded her visits to Aunt Phoebe's, where she was ordered to sit with her back as straight as an ironing board, walk around the house with books atop her head, and use her napkin after every bite. Aunt Phoebe seemed to be grooming Tilda for something, but Tilda wasn't sure what that something was. She never told Aunt Sippy, but she was always ready to leave Aunt Phoebe's house and return to While-a-Way Lane.

Even now, Tilda had a backache every time she

thought about Aunt Phoebe's worn-out, musty-smelly chair. She'd hoped Aunt Phoebe would leave her the shiny red wheelbarrow she never used instead. Aunt Phoebe didn't know Tilda at all.

After Aunt Phoebe's funeral, Tilda bought her own red wheelbarrow and hired a mover to relocate the chair to the attic. That way she didn't have to look at it every day.

Why not just give it away? you ask. What is in *your* attic? This and that and whatnots from dead ancestors, I suppose? Things you'll never use. What are attics for, anyway?

Zip and Zap loved Aunt Phoebe's chair. They chased each other around and under it. They bounced on the cushion like it was a trampoline. They played hide-and-seek, disappearing inside the holes. Yes indeed, the brothers thought Aunt Phoebe's chair was a very fine piece of furniture.

Tilda should have known something was up, but she'd been busy measuring her hosta, dusting its leaves, and trying to decide the exact moment to dig it up. She'd been shopping for a pot that would perfectly complement the large green leaves.

She'd been so tired from her busy morning she decided to take a little nap. She'd fallen fast asleep and slept so soundly (snoring a bit, too) that she didn't hear Zip and Zap racing over her head.

The brothers had discovered all kinds of treasures in the attic. They loved pretending Tilda's grandfather's fireman helmet was a boat, and they rocked inside, rapidly back and forth.

"We're pirates," said Zip.

"No, no," said Zap. "We're sailors." Zap always liked being a good guy.

"Pirates!" said Zip.

"Sailors!" said Zap.

The hat rocked and rocked.

Zip, the pirate, slid down to Zap's side, and Zap, the sailor, fell overboard and landed in an ocean of teacups and saucers.

The loud clatter caused Tilda to awake with a gasp.

She sat up. She got out of bed and shoved her feet

into her fuzzy bunny slippers with the floppy ears. If only the shovel wasn't outside in the potting shed. Frantic, she glanced around the room for a weapon and settled on Aunt Sippy's book called *Every Plant in the World*. Since there are a lot of plants in this world, the book was very thick and very heavy. Tilda believed it was guaranteed to make a big bump on someone's head.

With the book in her hands, she headed toward the stairs. When she stepped on the first one, the squeak traveled up to the attic.

Zip and Zap froze. "Uh-oh!" said the pirate and the sailor.

They hid under a white tablecloth, staying as quiet as two squirrels possibly could.

Zip began to jibber. Zap began to jabber. When they heard another squeak, they stopped.

Tilda took one more step. Then *she* stopped. She'd lived in this house all her life, but she'd visited the attic only once. And that was enough. She had been a curious little girl, and that curiosity had led her there. But up there every creak seemed like someone was out to get you.

Ghosts perhaps?

Young Tilda hadn't stayed to find out. She'd left in a hurry and never returned.

Now Zip and Zap were waiting, under the tablecloth, to see what happened next.

On the third step, Tilda thought about turning around, but when she caught a glimpse of her reflection in the mirror, she reminded herself that she was not a scared little girl anymore.

She took a fourth step, then a fifth, sixth, seventh, and eighth. She took every step until she faced the attic door. Then she put her hand on the knob, took a deep breath, and turned it slowly.

CHAPTER NINETEEN

THE ROOF

FRED WAS JUST the sort of dog that would be the perfect Nana. Daniel was 100 percent sure of this. He thought about it all the way home from rehearsal. That dog had star quality. He was big, furry, and didn't bark too much. Yes sir, he was the right choice for the role. Mrs. Garcia would realize that as soon as she saw him, just like she did when she met those twins. Maybe Daniel wouldn't be Curly, but he would be the one responsible for finding the best Nana. His dad would be proud. Daniel decided right then and there, he'd invite him.

Now all he had to do was ask Tilda Butter if he could borrow Fred. He was surprised to see his mom home early. She told him she got off half a day because she had to work on Saturday. After he ate his snack, he stepped out of his house and headed toward Tilda Butter's home. Halfway there, he stopped. Not just because he suddenly realized it might be hard to convince her to lend him her dog, but because he saw a vine clinging to Tilda Butter's home.

The vine was as thick as a tree branch and it had green leaves and purple flowers dripping from it. The flowers smelled sweet too, like grape jelly. That was nice, but Daniel's gaze followed the vine all the way up to the roof, where it stopped. Now, that was a vine worth climbing. For a minute, he wasn't Daniel with divorced parents, living on a boring street. He was Jack from "Jack and the Beanstalk." He was going to see what was at the top of this vine. Maybe a golden goose?

He grabbed hold of the woody vine and slipped his foot into a sturdy loop. Then he tugged with all of his might. To his relief, the vine didn't fall. He stretched his arms high, and his hands choked the vine so hard he caused some of the petals to fall to the ground, but the vine still clung to the house. Up he went, until his chin was even with the roof. A moment later he was on top, standing tall, looking down on While-a-Way Lane. He could see everything—some boys playing kickball in a backyard, the Lemonade Girl stacking cups at her stand, and at the very end—the pond. The pond where he would soon be sailing his boat with his dad.

He looked over at his own backyard, where his mom was sweeping the porch. Ever since they moved, she seemed to love sweeping the porch. Whenever his dad called him, she'd go out there and sweep until long after Daniel had hung up the phone. Now he watched her move the broom across the concrete. It didn't look that dirty. How could it be, with all that sweeping? And then he looked closer. Still holding the broom, his mother pulled a wadded tissue out of her apron pocket, smoothed it open, and wiped her eyes.

CHAPTER TWENTY

HEROES

A DISAGREEMENT was taking place in the attic under the tablecloth. Zap thought they should stay hidden. A sailor waits.

But Zip was a pirate. A pirate attacks. He grabbed a corner of the cloth and headed across the floor and up the arm of Aunt Phoebe's chair. Zap, being the fine sailor, held strong, keeping his end anchored to the floor.

Meanwhile Tilda's firm grasp slowly moved the door-knob clockwise. When Tilda finally eased open the door, the white cloth appeared to be standing straight up. At that exact moment, a breeze blew in from the roof hole and the tablecloth flapped. And there was her grandfather's fireman helmet at her feet.

The book flew from her hands into the air, and Tilda hit the floor hard, landing flat on her back, nose pointing straight up. Aunt Sippy's garden book followed, smacking her in the forehead.

It is a very good thing that there are nosy people in the world. Especially when one of those nosy people comes in the form of a boy named Daniel. When Tilda awoke, it was to a voice asking, "Hey, what are you doing on the floor?"

Tilda opened her eyes. An eyeball stared down from the hole in the ceiling. Then it moved farther away and disappeared. The eyeball was replaced by a mouth. "I said, what are you doing down there?"

Now Tilda knew whom the eyeball and mouth belonged to. "How did you get on my roof?" she asked Daniel.

"Easy," he said. "I climbed that vine."

"My wisteria?"

Tilda's wisteria vine only bloomed a couple of weeks out of the year. She imagined the purple petals scattered on the grass, blowing in the wind, away from her cottage. She tried to rise up, but she felt woozy.

"Whoa," she said, quickly returning to the floor.

"Can't you get up?" Daniel asked.

Tilda felt the bump. "I think something must have hit my forehead."

"I can get you up," Daniel said. "I'm strong."

"Oh?"

"I'm real strong," he said.

"I'm sure you're strong, but not enough for me."

A bark came from downstairs, followed by some whining. Fred!

"Oh dear," Tilda said. Fred had not been out since that morning, and she had no idea how much time had passed since she'd fainted. "Fred needs to go out. Can you do that?"

"You bet!" Daniel said.

"Thank you!" Tilda called out. "There's a key under the welcome mat. If you unlock the door, you can let Fred out. Be careful!"

A moment later, she heard Daniel land on the ground with a thump.

Soon she heard the front door open and shut.

"Hello, Fred!" Daniel said. "Ready to go out?"

Then she remembered.

"Out back!" Tilda yelled. "Put Fred in the backyard!" The backyard had a fence that would keep Fred from roaming down While-a-Way Lane.

She heard a door open. "Out back," she said softly to no one.

"There you go, boy." The door slammed. Maybe it was the back door.

"How do you get up to the attic?" Daniel said.

"The stairs at the back of the kitchen!" Tilda's throat started to feel sore from the straining.

But then she heard him on the stairs. The squeaks came quickly and didn't sound scary.

Daniel was in front of her now, but he was looking

around the attic, taking in all the dusty items that had been placed there from generations past.

"I need some help." Tilda stretched her arm toward him.

His focus lingered elsewhere. Tilda's attic was fascinating.

"Please!" Tilda waved her hand.

Daniel flexed his grape-sized biceps. Then he grabbed hold and gave Tilda a strong yank.

"Ow!" she said, trying to sit. "Careful, now. My muscles aren't as young as yours."

Daniel grunted and pulled once more. Then he let go of Tilda's hand, and she was flat again.

"I'm strong, but I think you ate too much chocolate pudding or something."

Daniel moved toward the fireman's helmet across the room. When he reached it, he put it on. The helmet slid down over his eyes, and he raised it above his brows.

Suddenly Zip and Zap appeared from under the cloth.

"Hey, I know you guys!" Daniel said.

The brothers didn't stay. They scampered up the back of Aunt Phoebe's chair, skittered across a tennis racket, leapt on top of an armoire, made their way over to a high shelf, then jumped, escaping through the roof hole.

Tilda frowned after the squirrels' tails. "I should have suspected mischief."

She rubbed her forehead. Her back was starting to hurt, too. She wondered how long she'd been on the floor. "You did let Fred out in the *backyard*, right?"

"Nope," Daniel said, tilting the helmet back on his head, admiring himself in the armoire's mirror. "I might be a fireman when I grow up."

"You let Fred out front?" Tilda asked weakly.

"Yep." Daniel pretended he was holding a fire hose. Then he dropped his arms to his sides like a soldier. "Or a police officer. I might be both. My dad said I could be anything I wanted when I grew up."

Tilda remembered the time she left the front door ajar while she positioned the soaker hose. Fred slipped out and romped around the neighborhood. He stayed away for hours. She had worried herself sick about him. When he returned later, she'd not even scolded him for getting out.

The boy looked up at the ceiling. "Why don't you fix that hole?"

"If I'd known there was a hole, I would have had it fixed."

"It might rain."

"It might," Tilda muttered, still flat on her back, thinking of Fred roaming the streets, dodging cars, getting lost. She could do nothing about it. How does one get out of these situations? She was about to ask Daniel to get his mother when she heard a knock and a bark.

Could it be?

Then another bark.

Yes, it was!

"Fred!" Tilda yelled.

"Yoo-hoo!" a voice came from downstairs. "Tilda Butter?"

"I'm up here!" she called out to . . . who on earth? She had no idea.

She heard eight squeaks. A second later a figure stood in shadows, a short figure with a perfectly round head. When he stepped forward, sunlight beamed down through the hole in Tilda's ceiling, shining on Dewey Wonder.

Dewey rushed over to her and knelt. "Oh, dear Tilda, are you hurt?" he asked without one stammer.

"She can't get up," Daniel said. He'd found an old microscope and was busy peering through its lenses.

Tilda touched the spot on her forehead. "I have a big bump on my noggin."

Then Dewey Wonder, who did not seem the strong type at all, took hold of Tilda's hands and pulled with all his might. Beads of sweat broke out on his face. He pulled again until Tilda was on her feet.

She took a wobbly step.

"Steady." Dewey was still holding her hand.

"Can you help me, young sir?" he asked Daniel, who was still staring through the microscope.

"Young sir?" Dewey repeated.

Daniel finally looked up. "Who, me?"

"Yes," Dewey said.

Daniel left the microscope and took hold of Tilda's other arm. "Why are you calling me *sir?*"

"What's your name?" Dewey asked.

Tilda beat Daniel to it. "He can't say. He's not allowed to tell strangers."

Dewey's eyebrows knitted, and Tilda knew what he was thinking. The boy was not allowed to share his name, but he could dig around in a stranger's attic. It was then that she noticed Daniel was wearing her grandfather's Purple Heart medal.

"Now, move slowly, Tilda," Dewey said. "We can't have you fainting."

"Yes," Tilda said, "that's how I bumped my head."

"Take small steps." Dewey guided her. Then he told Daniel to go downstairs and watch them climb down. "Make sure Miss Butter's feet land safely on each step. I'll be right behind her."

Daniel took off and said, "Okay, I'll catch her if she falls."

"Goodness pudding," Tilda muttered. She sure hoped that wouldn't happen.

Dewey led Tilda to the stairwell, and only when he knew she had a good grasp of the rail did he let go.

Tilda felt helpless and well taken care of at the same time. It was an unusual feeling for her. She rather liked it.

She took each step down the stairs to where Daniel and Fred waited.

Fred whimpered and wagged his tail. At first Tilda thought he was happy to see her and to know that she was okay. Then she realized Fred was waiting for his bowl to be filled.

Once all the way downstairs, she fed him. Then she made hot cocoa for Dewey and Daniel. They sat quietly around the kitchen table. Tilda watched Daniel running his tongue around the upper edge of the mug. *He is just a harmless boy,* she thought.

Then she asked Dewey, "How did you know I needed help?"

"I saw Fred wandering a few doors down. Thank

goodness I had some Woof Woof Wafers in my jeep."

"That's very smart of you, Dewey Wonder," she said. "Very smart indeed."

Dewey gazed at the little bump on Tilda's forehead like it was a beautiful pearl.

Tilda felt her cheeks prickle when she suddenly realized how very handsome Dewey Wonder looked in his uniform.

Daniel gazed up from his now empty mug. "Or I might be a mailman. Then I could rescue ladies in their attics who can't get up after they eat too much chocolate pudding."

It didn't matter what Daniel said. Tilda was not listening to him, and neither, did it seem, was Dewey.

CHAPTER TWENTY-ONE

DOG WALK

SATURDAY AFTERNOON Daniel knocked on Tilda Butter's door.

When she opened it, he asked, "Can I walk Fred?"

A bandage with ladybugs on it covered the bump on her forehead.

"Can I?" he asked again.

She looked back at Fred. "Well . . ."

Even at the front door, Daniel could see Fred staring at the terrarium.

"I'll hold on to his leash," Daniel said. "I promise I won't let go of it."

A moment later, she snapped the leash to Fred's collar and handed it to Daniel. "Watch him carefully. Don't go too far. And don't stay away long."

Daniel took hold and pulled.

Fred sat.

"Come on, Fred!" Daniel kept pulling.

Fred sprawled out on the floor. He looked like a shaggy rug.

Tilda Butter fixed her hands on her hips. "Fred, be a good fellow and get up. Go for a walk. Fresh air and sunshine will be good for you."

Daniel yanked at the leash, but Fred yanked back, dragging Daniel toward the terrarium. Then he saw what was capturing Fred's attention.

"Hey, there's a snail in there!"

"Yes," said Tilda Butter, "that's Snail. Such a little thing, but she can put away an entire head of lettuce. Always saying, 'More, more, more, please.'"

"Really? The snail talks?"

Tilda Butter didn't answer.

Daniel moved in closer. He sure wished he hadn't thrown Snappy into the donation box. He tapped on the glass. "Snail, say, 'More, more, please.'"

"She's not a parrot," Tilda Butter said, and walked away.

Fred watched Tilda with great interest. When he heard her lift the lid of the Woof Woof Wafer jar, he pulled toward the kitchen, but this time the boy let go of the leash.

Daniel squatted until his face was in front of the terrarium. "Hi, Snail," he said. "You look like Snappy."

Snail's antennas moved, and Daniel knew she'd heard him. "You know what, Snail?" he whispered. "Sometimes I'm still scared."

Tilda Butter walked out of the kitchen with a Woof Woof Wafer. She snapped it in half and offered one to Fred. "Here's the deposit. Go for a walk, and you'll earn the second half." She gave the remaining piece to Daniel.

Fred made a small sound like a mouse squeak. This was not the usual deal.

Daniel took full advantage now that Fred was standing. He grabbed hold of the leash, turned around, and headed toward the door with the second half of the wafer tucked in his pocket. He opened the door to leave with Fred, but not before saying, "Bye, Snail!"

"Remember what I told you," Tilda Butter said before the door closed.

Great things can happen when you put a dog and a boy together. They can have adventures. Daniel felt like he was a detective heading on his way to solve a mystery, or maybe a pirate with his first mate, or an explorer with an elephant comrade.

Until he heard "Yoo-hoo! Don't forget Freddie's bag, in case he does his business."

Daniel ignored her. He had somewhere to go, and he was already late. He heard Tilda Butter's shoes clicking on the sidewalk behind him. He walked a little faster, and because he had the Woof Woof Wafer in his pocket, Fred sped up, too.

"Daniel, stop!" Tilda Butter hollered.

From somewhere nearby a horn played out one long note. It seemed to be coming from Agatha Brown's house.

Daniel halted and swung around.

Tilda Butter was bent over, trying to catch her breath.

"What was that?" he asked.

"A saxophone, I think," Tilda said. Then Agatha Brown's window slammed shut.

"Hey, how do you know my name?" he asked.

Tilda Butter straightened. "Do you think I would let you walk my dog when I didn't even know your name?"

"But how did ya?"

"I guess I'm magic," she said. "So only walk Fred around the block, or I will turn you into a tulip bulb and plant you in my garden."

"Really?" Daniel was impressed. He moved toward her.

"Or a cat. Fred doesn't like cats."

"How about a horse? I'd love to be a horse."

She handed the bag to him and said, "Just get Fred back safely."

Daniel took the bag, and off he went with Fred. Was Tilda Butter magic? Did she really talk to snails, lizards, and snakes? Did they talk to her? Maybe she would turn him into a horse when he brought Fred back. Plus she would be so excited when he told her the good news about Fred being Nana in the play. But first he had to get to school.

FRED APPRECIATED the small things in life, like ants that gathered on the sidewalk where someone had dripped ice cream. And that meant he quit walking and watched.

"What are you stopping for, buddy? Do you need to do your business?" Daniel waited with the bag open.

But Fred just poked his nose at the ants.

This wasn't working as smoothly as Daniel had hoped. He patted his pocket.

"Remember the Woof Woof Wafer, Fred."

And at the mention of that, Fred lost interest in the ants, sat up straight, and barked.

Daniel was in charge again! They passed yard after yard, but to Daniel they were traveling across oceans and passing ships. He was a spy, after all. He noticed everything. They passed the lemonade stand, where a new sign stated OPENING SOON, BUY A LEMONADE AND SAVE THE MONARCH BUTTERFLY.

The porch light hanging loose from a house was a telescope from an enemy ship. A moment later, Daniel got on all fours and crawled next to Fred, who stopped and gave him a good sniff over.

"You must smell your reward," Daniel said. "You'll get that at the end of the walk."

Daniel had almost forgotten where they were going. He stood and took off. "Come on, Fred! They're after us."

No reason they couldn't have fun getting there.

Daniel sprinted, and Fred waddled as quickly as possible. He couldn't let his Woof Woof Wafer get away. When they made it to the corner, Daniel stopped for a quick break.

Fred flopped, but the boy wouldn't let him rest. They were off again.

A sprinkler system was spitting water on a yard, and Daniel led Fred zigzagging through the water. "Wow, that was close!"

The boy was so quick, he managed to only get a few sprinkles on his head, but Fred's timing was not so lucky. A big spurt of water had splashed him, soaking Fred from ear to tail. He tried to get in a good shake, but the boy hurried on.

DANIEL WAS IN A HURRY. He had to make it to another rehearsal of *Peter Pan*. Thank goodness the school was around the block. He turned and passed the library, but stopped to watch the kids on the Ferris wheel. Most of them were reading books. *That's dumb*, he thought.

A skinny guy with a newsboy cap was attending the ride. "Wanna spin?" he asked. "Your dog can ride, too."

"Nah," Daniel said, "I've got to go somewhere."

He started to leave, then asked, "Hey, why do all those people read books on the Ferris wheel?"

"Why not?" the guy said. "It's as good a place as any."

Daniel left him, but he still thought it was dumb.

Soon he was opening the front door to the school and making his way down the main hall toward the auditorium.

Fred left a trail of wet paw prints on the shiny floors. He needed to shake something bad, but the boy was walking so fast he could hardly keep up, let alone shake.

When they got to the auditorium, some of the other kids were already onstage. Mrs. Garcia sat in the front row with her back to Daniel and Fred. The boy playing Peter and the girl playing Wendy were saying their lines, but quit in mid-sentence when they saw Daniel and Fred entering the room. Wendy put her hand over her mouth, and Peter Pan laughed and pointed at Daniel.

Mrs. Garcia turned around. Her mouth opened, but no words came out.

"I found a Nana for you," Daniel announced. "His name is Fred."

Mrs. Garcia got up and walked toward him. She took a deep breath and said, "Daniel, we have a Nana."

"Yeah," said a girl, pulling off a mop-string dog

head and bonnet. Bobby pins flattened her black curls against her scalp. It was the Lemonade Girl. "I'm Nana!"

Then a taller girl said, "And I am, too!" She was wearing a pair of shaggy pants with a long tail.

Mrs. Garcia stepped closer to Daniel and lowered her voice. But she spoke firmly. "Dogs are not allowed at rehearsals."

As soon as she said that, Daniel lowered the leash and dropped it.

Have you ever had an itch that you just had to scratch? That's what it was like for Fred, who needed to shake himself dry. And that is exactly what he did.

He shook. And shook. He splattered Daniel, who didn't mind at all. He splattered Mrs. Garcia, who did.

"Take the dog home!" she said, wiping her eyeglasses with her sleeve. "Then come back here as soon as possible if you still want to be in the play."

Every person onstage was staring in his direction. The Lemonade Girl looked away like she was embarrassed for him. A big lump was stuck in his throat. He turned and led Fred out of the school and started the journey back to the yellow cottage.

He wondered why Mrs. Garcia couldn't see what a fine Nana Fred could be. Those two girls didn't look like a dog. If Fred could have gotten the part in the play, he could have told his dad that he was the reason Nana was a real dog. But now that wasn't going to happen. He wished he'd been Curly. Strep throat was spreading around school. Maybe Leonard, the kid who was playing Curly, would get strep throat and Mrs. Garcia would ask Daniel to play the role.

When they made the corner onto While-a-Way Lane, a strong barbecue aroma drifted out to the sidewalk. Daniel's and Fred's noses raised, taking in a big whiff. Daniel noticed the smoke coming from some ribs on a grill in one of the yards they were approaching. No one was out there, and for a moment, Daniel could imagine his dad flipping burgers. He did it every Fourth of July. His mom would spread a tablecloth on the grass, and they would have a picnic. He got so caught up in that memory that he loosened his grip on the leash and let go.

Fred bolted.

You know where. Toward the scent that was tantalizing his nose, making his mouth salivate, causing his stomach to rumble—the ribs.

"Scitter bum!" Daniel yelled. Then he sprinted after Fred.

It was too late.

Fred seized the ribs with his teeth, pulled them off the grill, and headed down While-a-Way Lane. The ribs flopped like the wings of a bird trying to take off, but they weren't getting away from Fred. The dog who could hardly keep up earlier was running the race of his life, dragging his leash behind him. He cut through two yards and their water sprinklers, getting drenched all over again. Nothing could stop him.

Daniel was yards away. Tilda Butter stood out front, watering her lilac bush, when Fred met her with his prize. "Goodness pudding, Fred! What do you have—"

To Fred's delight, Tilda dropped the hose, rushed over to the front door, and opened it.

Daniel saw her take a quick look around as if to make sure no one had noticed the crime. Then she followed Fred and slammed the door behind her.

Fred rushed past her into the house, stopped, and shook his body, splashing her and making puddles on the floor. Then he took his dinner to his favorite spot in front of the terrarium and watched Snail as he began to chow down on the ribs.

When Daniel finally reached Tilda Butter's cottage, he was out of breath. He thought about returning to school, but he didn't want to miss this chance to be something special. Something to impress his dad when he visited. He knocked on the door.

Tilda Butter opened it. She did not look happy. "Is there anything you want to tell me?"

She did not sound happy either, but Daniel asked anyway.

"Can you really turn me into a horse?"

CHAPTER TWENTY-TWO

TILDA REMEMBERS

"**T**URN HIM INTO A HORSE! Silly boy. Who does he think I am? A fairy godmother?" Tilda was not in a good mood. Fred was wet and smelly as an old mop. She had not given Daniel a chance to explain before saying goodbye and closing the door on him.

"The boy is scared," said Snail.

"How do you know?" asked Tilda.

"He told me."

Tilda thought about that the rest of the day. She got so consumed thinking about it, she washed every dish in her sink, did three loads of laundry, and much to Snail's delight, dropped a whole head of lettuce into the terrarium.

She even forgot that she needed to dig up her hosta. The Falling Star Valley Garden Show was soon. But her mind was on just Daniel. Yes, he was a peculiar boy, but he had heart. She knew this the moment she saw him trying to fix the broken irises.

When she remembered the hosta, she stepped out back to the oak tree with her shovel and the blue pot she had finally decided on. Somehow the hope of winning and riding on the float didn't seem that important now. She left the hosta in the ground until the day of the show.

There was a rustling sound at her feet.

"The boy'ssss mother doesssn't get home until dinner." Isadora was coiled up, shading herself under one of the prized hosta's leaves. This time Tilda did not startle because she had been in such deep thought about Daniel that it seemed Isadora had slid into her mind.

"That must make for one lonely boy," Tilda said. She

knew what that was like. She reached way back and remembered how even after Aunt Sippy welcomed her, it had been a scary time not knowing what was ahead.

Tilda remembered her first night, when she rode her little scooter down the street. She'd pushed off with one foot and made her way down the lane, passing cottage after cottage until she discovered the pond.

And then it happened. Something she had forgotten because it was so long ago. *The fireflies!*

CHAPTER TWENTY-THREE
THE LEMONADE GIRL

DANIEL RUSHED BACK to the school auditorium for the remainder of the rehearsal. He tried to forget about how Fred would have been a great Nana, how he was only Lost Boy #8, and whether or not to invite his mom and dad.

Most of the rehearsal he sat backstage waiting for the moment when Mrs. Garcia would announce, "Scene with lost boys!" And then when she finally did, it didn't change the way he felt, because he didn't have any lines.

While Peter Pan and Captain Hook said theirs,

he gazed around the stage until he noticed a stack of crates. They were part of the scenery, but no one was using them. What a waste! Someone should climb on top of them and jump. Suddenly he knew who that someone should be. Lost Boy #8!

He was standing at the back of the set, but he inched his way until he was close enough for his fingertips to reach the crates. His feet began to prickle. They were getting ready to make the climb when Mrs. Garcia said, "Lost Boy #8, you need to return to your spot."

Daniel couldn't understand how she, the director, could miss such a great opportunity. If he hadn't had a bad morning with the whole Fred episode, he would have spoken up and suggested it. Instead, he did what Mrs. Garcia told him to do and went back to his space, thinking about all the things that wouldn't happen that could have. He would just wait until the performance to make the jump. He got so excited about the idea. An idea that was special. Special enough for his dad to see the Champ do.

After rehearsal, the kids hurried out of the auditorium and exited the school. Some crawled into cars while others raced toward home. Daniel was in a hurry, too. He wanted to invite his dad to the play before his mom got home.

His mom wouldn't be home for another hour. She promised him this was the only Saturday she'd work but she had to go to orientation to learn about the new company she was working for. He wondered what her new job was, anyway. Then he remembered she'd told him, but he hadn't been listening.

She'd left out a movie and told him he could have all the microwave popcorn he wanted as long as he saved room for the lunch she'd made ahead for him. He sure hoped she wouldn't quiz him about the movie. Maybe if he hurried, he could watch part of it before calling his dad. He ran past the library and didn't even bother to look up to see who was on the Ferris wheel. He sprinted until he made it around the corner to While-a-Way Lane.

There, a few yards in front of him, was the Lemonade

Girl. He'd heard Mrs. Garcia call her Annie. She walked slowly, and so he slowed his pace. When she stopped, he did too.

Annie pulled a magnifying glass from her backpack and examined something in the grass. Daniel almost rushed up to her to ask if he could see, but he remembered how upset she'd been with him earlier. He guessed he couldn't blame her since he wanted Fred to take her part. Daniel forgot all about racing home and hung behind, waiting to see what she did next.

She took her time. Finally she tucked the magnifying glass into her backpack and picked up her pace, not stopping until she came to the lemonade stand. When she did, she reached under the table and pulled out a piece of cardboard and a marker.

Now Daniel had no choice but to pass her.

Or maybe he would stop.

He decided to stop.

"Are you mad at me?" he asked.

Annie didn't look up from her writing. "No."

She said it like she was a little mad. And how did she

know it was him, anyway? She must have known he was behind her the whole time.

"What are you writing?" he asked.

She finished the sign, then turned it around for him to read.

DUE TO A THEATRICAL PERFORMANCE, THE LEMONADE STAND WILL BE CLOSED UNTIL NEXT WEEKEND.

He read the other sign that she was replacing. He'd seen it before. BUY A LEMONADE. SAVE THE MONARCH BUTTERFLIES.

"What's wrong with the monarch butterflies?"

"They're endangered." Annie reached down into the box under the table and pulled out a stack of signs. She flashed the cards in front of him. "And so are the bumblebee, gorilla, hummingbird, red wolf, and . . ."

On and on she went, flipping the cards, spouting off animals and insects, some he'd never heard of.

The Lemonade Girl was going to save the world, one lemonade at a time.

She was smart. Daniel could plainly see that. She had big plans, bigger than any of his.

"How do you know all of that?" he asked.

Annie raised her eyebrows. "I've read about it. It's easy to find out stuff when you really want to know."

He thought of telling her about the fireflies, but decided not to. She might make it sound like it wasn't that special, and it had been. Meeting the fireflies had been the most special thing that had happened to him since he moved to While-a-Way Lane. It had been the only special thing.

CHAPTER TWENTY-FOUR

THE FIREFLIES

MANY YEARS BEFORE Daniel had ever heard of While-a-Way Lane, long before he was born, the fireflies had made young Tilda feel special, too.

Tilda was scared the day she watched her parents walk away from the yellow cottage. She stared at their backs, wondering what life would be like without seeing her mother practicing her bows and throwing kisses to the mirror. Or how she could spend an afternoon without hearing her father rehearse songs in his deep baritone voice while he stood in front of the parlor's open window. His daily ritual caused every neighbor to slam their windows shut, but that didn't stop him. Her father seemed quite pleased with the quality of his voice, always ending each session with "Bravo, good chap!"

She also wondered what life would be like without a party every night and all the people who attended and stayed until dawn—the trapeze artist who swung from their chandelier, the man who could play the harp and oboe upside down (at the same time), the couple who had been all around the world and spoke seventeen languages. There had been many fascinating people. She knew this because if they could not find anyone to speak with at the party, they settled next to little Tilda and started the conversation with "You may not know this, but I'm a fascinating person."

Her parents never gave her a bedtime, so every night she roamed the halls of their massive home and usually fell asleep under a skirted table, listening to the music and laughter. Back then, on that first day at the cottage, she thought about all of those things and wondered how she would do without them. It was the only life she'd ever known.

Hardly any time passed before Tilda found out that she would do just fine without them. She would do much better than fine on While-a-Way Lane because something much better than fine happened one night when she was on her scooter and discovered the pond. As if being out in the cool night air with the frogs croaking and the scent of lilacs weren't marvelous enough.

A flicker of light seemed to come from nowhere. Then two, three. Then a hundred, maybe a thousand. The fireflies surrounded her in such a way that it felt like a hug.

Have you ever been hugged by fireflies?

If so, then you know a gift follows those who receive an embrace touched by a thousand lights. The gift does not come packaged like a present with a big bow. No, it's not the kind of gift you will forget by your next birthday. It is an unexpected gift that will last a lifetime.

A few weeks after the fireflies incident, young Tilda noticed a lizard sunbathing on Aunt Sippy's front porch. She had never seen a lizard, so she bent over close to him and said, "Hello, Lizard!"

Then the lizard raised his head, tilting it to the right, and said, "Hello, Tilda Butter."

CHAPTER TWENTY-FIVE

EIGHT IS BETTER THAN SIX

Daniel threw peanuts to the two squirrels like he did most mornings. His plan to step closer and closer was working. Now they let him get ten feet away before they scampered off.

After his mother left for work, he locked up the house and headed toward school. He should have been excited because before his dad said goodbye on the phone the other day, he told Daniel he was coming to the play. For some reason, though, there was a knot in his stomach.

He had gotten halfway down the lane when he heard "Wait up!"

It was Annie.

Daniel's heartbeat raced, one thump tripping over another. He'd never felt that before. He hoped he wasn't having a heart attack. He tried to say hello, but he couldn't speak.

"Are you ready for the play?" she asked.

"I don't have any lines to learn."

"Well, your role is important. *Peter Pan* would hardly be worth seeing if there weren't any lost boys in it."

He didn't remind her that there weren't supposed to be eight lost boys.

The magnifying glass stuck out from a side pocket of her backpack. "Do you like living on While-a-Way Lane?"

"It's okay," Daniel said.

"Have you been down to the pond?"

Daniel nodded. "My dad and I are going to sail a boat together there after the performance."

"A *real* sailboat?"

"No," Daniel said. The pond wasn't that big. Maybe she wasn't smart about everything. "A remote-driven one."

Annie smiled. "Oh, a small one?"

"Yep. He bought one for me in Paris. That's where he is now. But he'll be back in time."

"Is your mom coming to the play, too?"

There, Daniel thought, that was why he had a knot in his stomach.

He shrugged and was relieved that they'd reached the school.

"Your mom is pretty," she said. "Does she ever make you waffles?"

"Sometimes."

"And does she ever put notes on napkins in your lunch?"

"Yeah." She was full of questions.

"My mom used to make me waffles and put notes on my napkins, too. Sounds like my mom was a lot like yours. See you at rehearsal!" Then she took off running up the steps to the school, taking them two at a time.

Daniel watched her walk through the front door, wondering if she would ever let him look through her magnifying glass.

DANIEL WAS NOT LISTENING closely enough. If he had been, he would have heard the *was* in Annie's reference to her mother. For it's true. Her mom was a lot like Daniel's. She made waffles, wrote notes on napkins, and rode bikes very slowly so she could see all there was to see. But Annie's mother was no longer in this world. Now it was just Annie and her dad. He was an absentminded college professor, sometimes wearing one brown shoe and one black shoe to work, and often forgetting where he'd put the eyeglasses that rested on top of his head.

He loved his daughter very much, but did not know how to make waffles and never had the notion to write a note on any napkin. In spite of all of this, Annie, the Lemonade Girl, was happy. It didn't occur to her to be any other way.

AFTER SCHOOL, Daniel dashed off to the auditorium.

There were only a few more rehearsals. He thought about what Annie said about the lost boys. She was right. How could Peter Pan fight Captain Hook and his pirates without the lost boys? The more he thought about it, he did have an important role. Eight lost boys *were* better than six.

Onstage, he studied the stack of crates again. He pictured himself climbing to the top and leaping off. Maybe he would even help Peter Pan fight Captain Hook. Mrs. Garcia's face flashed in his mind. Nah, he'd just stick with the big jump at the show performance.

Daniel played the scene over and over again in his head. He couldn't wait until Saturday, when his dad would watch him up there onstage. He would be awesome. If only he could figure out what to do about his mom.

CHAPTER TWENTY-SIX

A SECRET

WHEN THE LIZARD SPOKE to young Tilda, she was frightened. How would you feel if a lizard said hello to you?

A day later Tilda heard a bunch of mumbling at her feet. She squatted and parted the grass blades, only to find an army of ants carrying a dead beetle upside down. The ants all talked at once as they marched. Tilda leaned in and listened very carefully to hear what they had to say.

"This way!"

"No, that way!"

"This will make a fine dinner!"

"Lunch!"

"How much farther?"

"Where did we leave that hill?"

"I'm hungry!"

"Not as hungry as me!"

Their voices mixed together until they stirred into a loud buzz. Tilda covered her ears. Who knew ants could be so noisy? A few minutes later, a chickadee flew up and rested on a holly branch near the front porch.

"Are you Tilda Butter?" the chickadee asked.

Tilda looked around. "Yes," she said cautiously.

The chickadee paced back and forth on the branch. "Oh, I knew it, I knew it, I knew it!"

Then the rest of her family swept down and joined her. "This is Papa, Momma, and Cracker."

"Hello," Tilda said.

"Hello!" said the three chickadees.

"And who are you?" Tilda asked.

"I'm Pip-Tweet."

Young Tilda wasn't so frightened. She loved birds and always wondered what it would be like to fly. And now someone could tell her.

She asked her new acquaintance, expecting Pip-Tweet to say floating in air, or free as a breeze.

But Pip-Tweet answered her with a question. "What's it like to walk?"

That day, Tilda promised to keep what had happened to herself. No one would ever be able to understand anyway, so she would never, ever tell it. Except to one person.

When her aunt tucked her in that night, she whispered, "I have a secret."

"Oh?" Aunt Sippy whispered back.

"I can talk to birds and ants and lizards."

And instead of saying what any practical adult might say, Aunt Sippy had smiled and said, "Oh, Tilda, you have found your gift."

Tilda had not thought about that day for many years. She had been so busy trying to be just like Aunt Sippy that she had not appreciated her own gift.

"A gift is not to be wasted," Aunt Sippy had said.

Now she wondered, had she wasted hers?

CHAPTER TWENTY-SEVEN
THE KNOT

*P*ETER *P*AN WAS SATURDAY, only three days away. Daniel's dad told him he'd be arriving early that morning from Paris, but he'd be sitting in the front row when the performance started. Then he'd added, "You're the Champ," like he used to when they lived together in their old house.

When Daniel hung up the phone, he ran to his room and jumped on the bed eighty-six times. He would have jumped to a hundred if his mom hadn't hollered from her room for him to stop. Hearing her voice made that knot in his stomach come back.

Now all he could think about was his mom and how he'd kept the play a secret from her. It had been easy since the after-school rehearsals ended before she got home. The one Saturday rehearsal they'd had, she'd been at her job orientation. So Daniel hadn't really lied to her, but why did it feel like a lie?

If only it was like the old days when the three of them went everywhere together. But it wasn't. Every time his parents had been in the same room the last year, there'd been a lot of yelling. And his mom always ended up crying. He couldn't have that on the day he was Lost Boy #8.

He missed his dad. He missed him so much. His mom got to see Daniel every day. So wasn't it only fair that he could spend one day with his dad?

Daniel focused on his plan. His costume was in a sack tucked under his bed next to the box with his boat, waiting for the day to take place.

He would tell his mom he was going outside to ride

his bike, sneaking by her before she noticed the sack and box, and asked about it. He would have to use one hand to steer the bike, since the box would rest on the handlebars.

Later when he jumped off the crates, everyone would notice him instead of Curly. Especially his dad. Afterward, he and his dad would sail the boat at the pond. One thing he hadn't quite figured out, though, was how he would explain being gone all afternoon.

What could be the worst thing that happened? His mom would probably punish him. She might not let him ride his bike for a really long time.

Was that knot in his stomach ever going to go away? He sure hoped he wasn't getting sick. He stuck out his tongue and checked his throat in the mirror. Nope. No sign of infection. Maybe he'd go for a bike ride around the block.

Thinking about that made Daniel remember the fireflies. And that made him feel much better.

CHAPTER TWENTY-EIGHT

SOMETHING IN THE WIND

HAD TILDA WASTED her gift? She had never figured out why being able to communicate with every creature was important. Every creature except for one.

"I wish I could talk with Fred," she said aloud.

Hearing his name, Fred came over to her and settled at her feet. "Well, hello there, Fred. I finally got your attention." Tilda had made peace with having to share him with Snail now.

Fred rolled over on his back.

"Want your belly rubbed?" she asked him.

She gave him what he wanted and a pat on the head, too. Then a thought came to her. All these years she'd wondered why couldn't she talk to Fred, and the answer had been right in front of her. She already knew how to communicate with him. No need for her special gift to do that.

Tilda knew when Fred wanted his belly rubbed. She knew when Fred needed out, when he was hungry for dinner, or wished for a Woof Woof Wafer. She knew when Dewey Wonder was delivering the mail because Fred's actions told her.

The wind started to howl, and the bamboo chimes outside her front door rang.

She checked out the back window and was relieved her hosta was barely moving in the wind because the fence and oak tree were protecting it. The garden show was this Saturday.

Then Tilda looked out the front window. Some of the leaves on the magnolia tree fluttered to the ground, and the chickadee family flew to a high branch. She thought of Pip-Tweet and wondered if they were her descendants. For years her little friend had returned and nested in Aunt Sippy's holly.

The wind raged. The bamboo chimes fell and then a big gust of wind pushed them toward the street.

Tilda left her chair and went outside to try and retrieve them. Every step she took, the wind chimes moved farther away, finally stopping when they reached the mailbox.

The chimes seemed to be leading her to something or someone. And they were.

Poor Spider was holding on for dear life, each leg gripping and stretching as far as it could reach while the web flapped, looking as if it was going to snap off the mailbox frame at any moment.

"Oh, Spider!" Tilda said. "Are you okay?"

"Yes, Miss Butter." His voice came out rickety. "I must steer my ship and stay the course."

The wind had caused Tilda's hair to stand straight up, and her dress blew out like a parachute, but she was thinking only of Spider. "Why don't you come in for some hot tea until the wind has calmed down?"

"Tea?" Spider asked.

Tilda nodded, offering her palm.

Then Spider spun a thread of web around Tilda's finger and made his way to a safe harbor.

CHAPTER TWENTY-NINE

THE INVITATION

DANIEL NOTICED DEWEY WONDER driving away from his home, so he dashed outside to the mailbox. Maybe his dad had sent him a postcard from Paris.

There was no postcard. It didn't matter. Daniel would see his dad soon. If his dad said he'd be back in time for the play, he would.

Tilda Butter waved to him from her yard. Maybe she wasn't mad at him anymore. "Good day, Daniel! Would you like to take Fred for a walk?"

She *wasn't* mad.

"Sure!" He dashed across the grass and leapt over her circle of pink flowers.

"Watch out for the tulips!" Tilda Butter hollered.

He missed them, of course. He was, after all, Lost Boy #8, the best jumper in the play.

"Come in while I get Freddie," she said.

Inside, Fred was watching Snail, but as soon as Tilda Butter lifted the Woof Woof Wafer jar's lid, he wobbled off to the kitchen. While she gave Fred the rules about no sprinklers or barbecue stealing, Daniel moved in closer to Snail and told her, "I didn't invite my mom."

Snail moved her antennas, and when she did, a solution came to Daniel. Now he knew what to do. It came to him so quickly that it was as if Snail had told him. In a way she did, because he hadn't thought of it until he spoke to her.

He *would* invite his mom. He'd make an invitation and slip it under her pillow before he left for the play.

Like every morning, she would probably make her bed so early she wouldn't discover it until later, hopefully not until the end of the day, after the play was over and after his dad and he had sailed the boat. At least he would have invited her. He couldn't help it if she didn't know in time.

Tilda Butter had the leash snapped to Fred's collar, and Fred wagged his tail, focused on Daniel.

"Fred must really want to go for a walk!" Daniel said.

Daniel was right. Fred couldn't wait. A walk with Daniel meant the possibility of ribs.

Tilda Butter handed over the leash to Daniel. "If you bring him back in ten minutes, nice and dry, with no neighbors' dinner, there will be a cup of hot cocoa waiting for you."

"Deal!" Daniel headed with Fred to the front door. He turned around and asked, "Hey, you wouldn't happen to have any of that pie, would ya?"

"That gooey pie?"

Daniel nodded.

"Sorry," Tilda said, "not today."

"Aw, that's okay." Then he started the journey around the block, with his mind fixed on Saturday's plan while Fred's head turned right and left, scouting for barbecue grills.

CHAPTER THIRTY

A DATE

TILDA GLANCED AT THE CLOCK. Dewey Wonder would be arriving soon with the mail. It was the day before the Falling Star Valley Garden Show, and she had decided she would ask Dewey to attend the event with her. She wanted someone special there to clap when she won.

The mailbox was empty, so that meant she hadn't missed her chance to see him. She decided to wait. But she did not wait alone.

"Good afternoon, Miss Butter," Spider said. "Such a lovely time of day for tea, don't you agree?"

"I'm not in much of a mood for that today," Tilda said. "Although I enjoyed our tea the other day. I might get a lemonade a little later on, though."

"Not today," Spider said in his know-it-all tone.

"And why is that?" Tilda asked.

"The Lemonade Girl is at dress rehearsal for the school play. She's playing some beastly thing with a mop head."

"Oh." Tilda was disappointed.

"Yes, and so is the pest."

How had she missed all of this?

"When is the play?" she asked the know-it-all.

"Tomorrow. So perhaps today *is* a lovely day for tea?"

"What time?" Tilda asked.

"The traditional tea time would suit me. Four o'clock?"

Tilda sighed. "I meant the school performance."

"Pity." Spider sounded disappointed. "Two o'clock."

It was the same time as the garden show.

"How do you know?" she asked Spider.

"Who lives on While-a-Way Lane that wouldn't know? Every child passing by is buzzing about it. And their parents, too."

Tilda left Spider and headed to her back garden. She stared at the new blue pot next to her hosta. Then she walked to the toolshed, but instead of picking up the shovel, she grabbed her clippers. She cut the most perfect leaf from her hosta, went inside, and dropped it into Snail's terrarium.

Tilda joined Spider outside again. Dewey was at Daniel's mailbox and would be heading Tilda and Spider's way next.

"Oh!" groaned Spider. "Not him again! My web takes such a shaking every time he opens and shuts this box. I must leave before the quake. See you in a bit." Then he spun a thread and lowered himself to the ground.

"Toodle-oo!" Tilda said.

Dewey drove up to Tilda's box.

"Hello, Dewey. Do you have plans tomorrow afternoon?"

Dewey cleared his throat. "Nothing important except feeding my cat."

"How would you like to go to a play with me?"

CHAPTER THIRTY-ONE

THE PLAN

SATURDAY MORNING, Daniel's mom was in the backyard, planting flowers. Earlier she'd actually hummed while she was making his waffles. He couldn't remember the last time she'd hummed *or* made waffles. It had never happened on While-a-Way Lane. Daniel felt that knot in his belly again, knowing that he was keeping the play a secret. Then he reminded himself, he was going to invite her.

While his mom threw some sugar and flour into a

mixing bowl, he left the kitchen and slipped the invitation under her pillow. Just as he'd predicted, her bed was made. She wouldn't discover it until tonight.

At breakfast, his mom asked him questions about school. She wanted to know everything.

Daniel told her everything except about the play.

The morning dragged, and he watched the clock, wondering if his dad's plane had landed yet.

He wasn't even hungry when it was time for lunch, but he didn't want his mom to be suspicious, so he ate half of his sandwich and all of his potato chips.

Soon after, Daniel grabbed his costume sack and the box with his boat and sneaked out of the house. Then he opened the door and yelled, "I'm going out to ride my bike. See you later!"

He closed the door before she could say anything. Nothing could ruin his plan.

The two squirrels were out there scampering around in his yard, digging. With all the excitement of the day, he had forgotten to throw out some nuts for them. He didn't have time to do it now, though. Squirrels hid food all the time, so he hoped they'd find some without him.

Daniel tucked the sack inside his backpack and balanced the box in the middle of the handlebars. Then he pushed off with his right foot, heading toward school, one hand on the box and the other steering the bike. The handlebars wobbled. He wished he'd practiced. Halfway down the street, he thought maybe he should have walked. He was just trying to get away, unnoticed, as quickly as possible. Now he was worried about what his mom would think when he didn't come back for a few hours.

Right before the corner, Daniel slowed his pace and made the turn a little too sharply. The box fell. The boat tumbled out. He slammed on his brakes, lost his balance, and fell next to the boat. The mast and sail had broken off. His eyes stung, and he bit his lip to keep from crying. He lifted the pieces. The boat looked like a bat wing, dangling from his hand.

Laughter came from up the street. At first he thought they were laughing at him, but he discovered it was coming from the Ferris wheel. Stupid Ferris wheel!

A car slowed beside him, and someone rolled down the back window.

It was Annie. Her curls were pinned close to her head. "Are you okay?"

"Yes." Daniel jumped to his feet and brushed his hands off on his jeans. His face burned.

"What happened?" she asked.

"Nothing," Daniel snapped. Wasn't it obvious?

"Hey, is that the boat you were talking about?"

"It's broke," Daniel said.

"I'm sorry."

And Daniel could tell she really was.

"Maybe it can be fixed. See you at school."

She rolled up the window, waved, and her dad drove away.

It's all ruined, he thought, but then he remembered how his dad once fixed a broken toaster. He'd opened it up and put the toaster back together again. This wouldn't be as hard to repair as a toaster. After the play, they'd stop at a store and get some glue to fix it. Then they'd head to the pond.

Daniel decided not to chance another break. He hid his bike and boat in some bushes in front of the library and walked the rest of the way to school.

CHAPTER THIRTY-TWO

TILDA'S PLANS

TILDA HAD HER OWN PLANS for the day. They did not include going to the Falling Star Valley Garden Show or winning first place with her hosta. And that was fine by her. There was always next year. Besides, she probably wouldn't like riding in a parade anyway.

Her plans for this day were simple.

1. *Bathe Fred*
2. *Choose a hat to wear with her best dress*

3. *Wait for Dewey to pick them up for the play*

4. *Applaud loudly when Daniel came onstage*

Do you know what it is like to bathe a big dog that doesn't like water dripping into his eyes? Tilda knew and that is why she did it in the backyard. Out there, Fred could shake off the water to his heart's content.

While Tilda gathered Fred's shampoo and the huge metal tub, she thought about Daniel. She hoped the play was a sign that he was starting to feel at home on While-a-Way Lane. She grabbed the hose—at least she thought it was the hose.

"Excu*sss*e me, dear friend. Can't I s*ss*unbathe without being jarred awake?"

"Isadora!"

"Of cour*sss*e it'*sss* me. Who did you think it wa*sss*?"

Tilda didn't say a word. She was afraid Isadora might be offended by being compared to a hose.

"What i*sss* Fred getting all fancied up for?" Isadora asked.

"Daniel is in a play today."

"Oh yes*ss*, I remember."

"You knew, too?"

"I am a s*ss*nake."

Tilda realized that even though she might have been able to speak to almost every little creature on While-a-Way Lane, she still had a lot to learn about them.

A<small>N HOUR OR SO LATER</small>, Tilda was dressed in her red hat and polka-dotted dress. Fred had on his checked neckerchief. She only hoped Fred would not bark at Dewey. While they waited for him, Fred plopped on the grass and Tilda sat next to him, leaned in, and listened.

When Dewey drove up, it was as if he had never left that moment so long ago when he first saw young Tilda sitting on the grass and staring at the blades. This time he asked, "What are you doing?"

She was startled at being caught, but Tilda answered him with honesty. "Listening for ants."

After Dewey helped Tilda up, Fred stood on his hind legs, rested his front paws on Dewey's shoulders, and licked his face, neck, and arms. He was making his way to Dewey's belly when Tilda smelled Woof Woof Wafers, as if Dewey had dusted himself in them from his head to his toes.

CHAPTER THIRTY-THREE
THE PERFORMANCE

DANIEL PEEKED THROUGH the curtains. The play would begin in thirty minutes, and people had started to arrive, mostly parents. But his dad wasn't there yet.

A man came backstage carrying two bouquets of roses. They were from the parents of the girls playing Mrs. Darling and Wendy. Daniel checked through the curtains again. He looked at every seat. Except for Annie's dad, he didn't recognize one person in the audience. *Where was his dad?*

"Lost Boy #8, come away from the curtains."

Daniel let go. Each time she called him that, it reminded Daniel how he didn't have a real part in the play. He didn't even get to use his slingshot. He had to carry a silly bow with no arrow.

Another delivery worker came backstage with a box. "Daniel Peppergood!"

Daniel's heart pounded. "That's me!"

"Package for you." The delivery worker handed over the box.

Daniel opened it, and there inside under the tissue paper was another boat, a red one just like the blue one his dad had given him. How did his dad already know about the broken one? His dad had to be the smartest man in the world. He sifted through the tissue paper as if expecting to find his dad there. But the only other things inside were the boat's remote control and a note.

Daniel read it silently.

Dear Daniel,
I'm sorry I couldn't be with you today. The French deal had a glitch, and I had to stay longer to fix

it. I'm sending this boat to you because when I get back, I promise we'll sail the boats together. Now that we have two, we can race them. You're my best pal, Champ.

Love, Dad

PS Break a leg!

The other cast members gathered around him when they noticed the boat.

"Cool," said Peter Pan.

"Awesome!" said the twins at the very same time.

But Annie, who was holding Nana's head, looked at Daniel as if she knew how he really felt.

Daniel stared at the boat.

"Wow," said Mr. Darling. "I wish I had a boat like that."

"Here," said Daniel, "you can have this one."

"Really?"

"No, Mr. Darling," said Mrs. Garcia. "You can't have Lost Boy #8's gift. Now, if everyone would gather together for the cast circle."

Daniel hated this part where they stood in a circle holding hands. And he especially hated it today. He didn't feel like being in the play anymore. He would have felt that way right now even if he'd gotten the part of Curly.

While everyone made a huge circle and held hands, Daniel looked up at the black ceiling. Thick cords and lights crisscrossed above their heads. Maybe he could climb up there and escape. No one would miss him.

Something moved quickly across one of the cables. It was brown. Another brown thing scampered behind it. Daniel squinted his eyes, trying to see closer. Were those the squirrels that visited him every morning? One of the squirrels flicked his tail. Yes, they were his friends!

Then he saw a tiny light. And another. Yet another. The fireflies! It was the middle of the day, and here they were. His friends had come to see him in the play.

Mrs. Garcia was still yakking about what a great cast they were and how proud she was of them.

"Hello," Daniel mouthed to the squirrels and fireflies.

The squirrels flicked their tails. The fireflies twinkled against the dark ceiling.

Mrs. Garcia clapped her hands. "Okay. Everyone get in your places. Nana's Head, come away from the curtain."

Annie stepped back and turned around. "Your four-legged friend is out there," she told Daniel.

"Huh?" Daniel said, but then he realized she could be talking about Fred. Despite Mrs. Garcia's warnings, Daniel dashed over and peeked through the crack between the curtains.

It *was* Fred. He was sitting in his own seat next to Tilda Butter and Dewey Wonder. And next to them, at the end of the row, was someone he knew very well.

His mother.

CHAPTER THIRTY-FOUR

GIFTS

EVEN IF YOU have never been hugged by fireflies, you may have been lucky enough to have a mother. A mother like Daniel's mom. A mother who has a gift of knowing things instinctively. Oh, your mother may tell you she knows things because she has eyes in the back of her head, but she is only joking. Her gift has nothing to do with eyes.

It has everything to do with heart.

○ ○ ○

BEFORE DANIEL CHANGED out of his costume backstage, his mom caught him in the hallway.

"You were the best lost boy I've ever seen in *Peter Pan*."

"I was?" He hadn't even done the jump. Not because he was scared and not because he didn't think it was a great idea, but because once the curtains went up, it had seemed enough to be Lost Boy #8.

"I made a cake for you. We'll have some later at home. I thought we'd have Tilda and Dewey over. Fred, too, of course. Do you want to invite any of your friends?"

Daniel looked over at Annie, whose father was giving her a big hug. He knew exactly which friend he'd invite.

Before his mom left, he asked, "How did you know? About the play?"

"Oh, a little squirrel told me," she said and winked.

OUTSIDE THE SCHOOL, families waited for the cast. Daniel took a big breath and made his way through the sea of dads, moms, and grandparents. "Bravo, Daniel!" a familiar voice called out.

He swung around. His mother had not left yet. She was standing and clapping with Tilda Butter and Dewey Wonder.

"Bravo!" Tilda Butter said again.

"I just knew you'd jump off the crates," Dewey Wonder told him. "I was so surprised when you didn't."

"That would have been a good idea," Daniel said.

"A good idea for a broken bone," said Tilda.

"I spoke to your friend's dad," his mom said. "They're going to join us for cake."

Fred was wagging his tail. Then he opened his mouth as if he was about to bark and said, "Ribs! Ribs! Ribs!"

"See?" Tilda Butter said. "Fred thinks you did great, too."

Daniel couldn't believe it. Fred was talking to him.

"Ribs! Ribs!"

"Okay, Fred," Tilda Butter said. "That's enough! Stop barking."

"Did you hear what he said?" Daniel's heart pounded. He'd never known a dog who could talk.

"Ribs!" Fred said. Then he added a growl.

"I'll bet he wants you to take him for a walk," Tilda said. "Would you like a summer job doing that?"

Daniel nodded.

"We'll see you at your house," Dewey told him.

He watched the four of them walk away, wondering if his mind had played a trick on him. Then he remembered something. He turned back around and ran into the school to get his new boat.

CHAPTER THIRTY-FIVE

ON WHILE-A-WAY LANE

IF YOU LOOK CLOSELY you might see a lizard peering down from a branch above, a spider busy rebuilding his web after a storm, or fireflies twinkling against the night sky. And if you listen closely you might hear the song of chickadees returning in spring, a saxophone tune drifting from a neighbor's window, or even a teeny-tiny snail nibbling on a lettuce leaf. The art of noticing is the gift we all own.

IT WAS THE FIRST DAY of summer break and Daniel had an entire Ferris wheel seat to himself. He looked around at his world, swinging his feet back and forth.

"I can see my house and the stand," said Annie, who sat on the seat behind his.

Daniel could see all of While-a-Way Lane. Each time his seat met the sky, he searched for something new. He could spot Dewey Wonder's jeep making the stops at each mailbox.

Tilda Butter was in her yard pruning roses, while Fred barked at Dewey Wonder's cat, Stamps, who had climbed to an upper branch of the magnolia tree.

There was Daniel's bike, lying on the front lawn. He'd forgotten to put it up last evening. Just then his mom came outside and raised the bike upright. Instead of guiding it to the garage by the handlebars, she hopped on and took a spin in the driveway. She even went a little fast.

The next time his Ferris wheel seat was at the high-est point, he noticed the pond where he'd sailed the

boat with his mom the day after the play. They'd had a really good time, laughing when the boat ran into a stump in the middle of the pond. The next week he'd sailed the boat with his dad. They'd seen each other every weekend since then.

Annie and Daniel had been riding for twenty minutes, but the Ferris wheel on Wit's End stopped only when you wanted it to. Maybe they would ride all day.

Just then, Daniel heard music coming from his street.

"Look," Annie said.

He twisted around and discovered she was pointing at the piano teacher's house. Agatha Brown was perched on her windowsill, playing a saxophone solo. He kind of liked the bouncy tune.

"She looks happy," Daniel said.

"Yeah," said Annie, "she does."

It was funny, he thought, how today he noticed things from far away that he hadn't paid much attention to close up. Like how maybe Fred only barked at Dewey Wonder because he smelled like his cat, and how spending time with his mom could be as fun as with his dad.

Even little things became clearer looking closer from this high up. Until now, he'd never realized there was actually a *white* house on While-a-Way Lane. How had he missed that?

Daniel remembered climbing to the top of the tree at his old house, each branch taking him to a new adventure. Up here, at the top of the Ferris wheel, he felt like he did then. Like the Champ.

When the wheel lowered, he took a giant breath. The air smelled of cotton candy. To Daniel, it was the best-smelling air in the whole wide world.

ACKNOWLEDGMENTS

SOME WONDERFUL PEOPLE read part or all of this story and offered advice, support, or encouragement. Please know I am grateful for every bit of your input.

Thank you:

Christy Ottaviano, Shannon Holt, Alison Cheney, Amy Berkower, Brenda Willis, Ray Willis, Jessica Anderson, Jennifer Archer, Charlotte Goebel, Jane Shuffer, Martha Moore, Jeanette Ingold, Rebecca Kai Dotlich, Lola Schaefer, and Kathi Appelt.